THE EXECUTIONE

OTHER BOOKS BY EDWARD GLOVER

THE HERZBERG TRILOGY

The Music Book

A young English woman, on the run from her father, and a retired
Prussian military officer sent to England by King Frederick the Great are
plunged into the London demi-monde and a pursuit across Europe in
search of fulfilment. The young woman's music book bears witness to
what unfolds.

Fortune's Sonata

English by birth, Prussian by marriage, rebellious by nature, the beautiful
Arabella von Deppe steers her family through turbulent historical times
in this thrilling story of love and loss, betrayal and revenge, ambition and
beliefs, friendship and fate. With music as her inspiration and a murderer
as her friend, she proves a worthy adversary of Fortune as she weathers
winds beyond her control.

A Motif of Seasons

Two powerful 19th-century English and Prussian families are still riven
by the consequences of an ancestral marriage – one that bequeathed
venomous division, rivalry and hatred. Three beautiful women – each
ambitious and musically gifted – seek to break these inherited shackles of
betrayal, revenge and cruelty in their pursuit of sexual freedom and love.
But the past proves a formidable and vicious opponent.

The Executioner's House

EDWARD GLOVER

THE OAK HOUSE

Published by The Oak House
High Street, Thornham, Norfolk PE36 6LY

ISBN: 978-0-9929551-3-7

Do not tell secrets to those whose faith and silence you have not already tested.

Elizabeth 1

Great advantage is drawn from knowledge of your adversary, and when you know the measure of his intelligence and character, you can use it to play on his weaknesses.

Frederick the Great

CONTENTS

CHAPTER ONE

The Courtroom

The entrance to the plain-fronted building, set back from the main road, was architecturally unremarkable and still largely intact despite the intensity of Allied bombing in the latter part of the war. Passing the military guard, Major Richard Fortescue climbed a wide flight of stairs to the first floor. Turning left, he walked a few paces to enter a spacious high-ceilinged wood-panelled room with two large curtained windows high up on the right-hand side.

It was Thursday 24 October 1946. He had returned to the courtroom at Nuremburg where, between 20 November the previous year and 1 October, he had witnessed the trial, conviction and sentencing, for war crimes, of Hermann Göring, Rudolf Hess, Julius Streicher, Hans Frank, Wilhelm Frick, Alfred Jodl, Ernst Kaltenbrunner, Wilhelm Keitel, Joachim von Ribbentrop and fifteen other Nazis. He had seen the bodies of those who had been executed the week before. His job as an interpreter and legal assistant on secondment from the army to the British prosecuting team led by Sir Hartley Shawcross and his deputy Sir David Maxwell Fyfe was now done. It was time for him to say farewell to remaining colleagues and friends in the US, French and Soviet teams and leave for Berlin for some final duties and thereafter departure to London. Aged thirty-two, he was uncertain of his future.

There were few present in the courtroom that morning. It was being prepared for more prosecutions. Shafts of late-autumn sunlight penetrated between the curtains. On the left, facing the windows, was the dock where the accused had sat; beneath the windows was the bench where the judges, two each from the United States, the United Kingdom, the Soviet Union and France, had presided. In front of the accused had sat their German defence lawyers. The prosecutors had been to their right, the accused and witnesses testifying in front of them. In the far left-hand corner of the courtroom had sat the translators, providing simultaneous translation for the very first time.

Those in the courtroom that morning spoke in whispers. He absorbed the atmosphere one more time – a late-autumn warmth outside but the chill of death inside. As a cleaner silently swept the floor, he could almost hear the echo of the words of the accused at the start of the trial as each was asked to respond to the charge against them. "*Nicht schuldig,*" not guilty, was the frequent reply.

Fortescue recalled his urgent summons to Nuremburg in the late spring of the previous year; the rush to acquaint himself with the intended trial proceedings; his participation in the interrogation of some of the accused; hearing, with the commissioners appointed by the court, the harrowing evidence of the thirty-three witnesses who testified for the prosecution against the indicted; and spending countless hours sifting through the never-ending river of accumulated documentary evidence, some pages compelling in their distressing narrative while others were sickening in their grisly detail. A victim of long days and sometimes mixing with the hard-drinking international press corps in the evenings, including, occasionally, Rebecca West, writing for *The New Yorker* magazine, he had become a smoker and partial to late-night whisky, much to the admonishment of his girlfriend, Susannah, in her letters impatiently awaiting his return to London. He would never forget the written testimony, the grainy, gut-churning film of the concentration camps and the neat handwriting of each entry on page after page of the SS records, listing, like accomplished bookkeepers, those deported and executed. Nor would he forget the frequent nonchalance of some of the defendants during interrogation or in the dock – the way they smirked, seemingly oblivious to the enormity of the crimes they had committed.

After final goodbyes, he left the building without a backward glance and headed to what remained of the old city. He stopped, again for one last time, at the badly bombed thirteenth-century St Sebaldus Church, surrounded by rubble, its once beautiful nave still used for worship despite being open to the sky. He sat for a few minutes to ponder the destruction, the cost of war and the future. Within three weeks, he would be back in London. Leaving the church, he joined some American colleagues in a bar, eventually returning to his billet to pack his belongings and snatch a few hours' sleep.

Early the next morning he left by road for Munich, where he had decided to stay a day or so before flying in a military aircraft to Berlin. Though the Bavarian capital had suffered extensive Allied bombing, he hoped it would still be possible to revisit some of the places he had seen as a young man in the autumn of 1938, when he had stayed with a family in Wilhelm-Weitling-Straße, improving his German and surveying the literary landscape. The opera house, where he had seen Wagner's *Tristan und Isolde*, was now shattered but sight of its ruins would still bring back the memory of meeting, in the interval, a tall attractive blond girl in a low-cut dirndl. He and Annalise, whose family were devoted admirers of the Führer, had met several times afterwards and on his departure in December 1938 they promised to keep in touch, but she never replied to his letters – no doubt intercepted by her parents or by the police. He would try to find the seedy hotel where they had once spent a night together – he having sex for the first time.

CHAPTER TWO

The Girl in the Café

After a day walking around the ruins of Munich's old city and spending an evening with his American colleague and friend from Nuremburg, Max Steiner, who was on his way to join the US army war crimes unit in Berlin, Fortescue got up early the next morning. Returning once more to the city centre, he went to a café a stone's throw from the historic National Theatre which, until it was gutted in an air raid three years before, had been Bavaria's prestigious opera house. It was Saturday 26 October.

He sat by the window, drinking a large mug of unpleasant bitter-tasting coffee, watching people scurry past. Though the streets had been extensively cleared of debris, Munich remained a war-shattered city, beautiful landmark buildings still empty shells, stripped bare of the Nazi cultural veneer he had seen in 1938. Electricity supply was still erratic and heating at a premium. Its citizens had not regained their pre-war *joie de vivre*. Poorly dressed, they went silently about their business – whether legitimate or not. In the half-full café, no one spoke, each hunched over their meagre fare. In an atmosphere of little trust and boundless cynicism, people were careful what they said and to whom they said it. Max had described Munich as the city of the damned. He had countered that such a soubriquet was surely better reserved for Berlin. Max shrugged his shoulders.

Light snow began to fall, adding to the city's dismal profile. He glanced through some old newspapers on the windowsill, including an edition of *Der Tagesspiegel* of 6 October reporting the sentences passed at Nuremburg across which someone had scrawled an indecipherable expletive. Pushing them away, he opened his well-thumbed pre-war travel book about a journey to East Prussia in the 1920s – a journey he had wanted to make in 1938 but his money had run out, leaving only enough to get back to England for Christmas. The book contained some fine sepia photos of distinctive buildings – all of which, he imagined, the Russian army had demolished in their advance towards Berlin. He had found it in a street flea market the day before. Beneath it on the stall was a battered copy of *Mein Kampf*, now banned, with various passages underlined in black pen. He had bought the two at the asking price, taking pity on the shrivelled elderly stallholder shivering in the cold, telling her to keep the change. In return she had shown him a chipped ashtray bearing the Nazi emblem, which she hastily rewrapped in its newspaper before thrusting it into his hand – a bonus, she said, for his kindness. Leafing through *Mein Kampf* later, it appeared to be inscribed by a soldier in the *Wehrmacht*. Towards the back was a folded blood-stained swastika armband, perhaps used as a bookmark. At the end, someone had written "*Quatsch!*" What a load of rubbish!

He looked up. A young woman had entered the café. She was tall, slim with shoulder-length brown hair. She wore a shabby dark-green coat, its hem above the knee, and a fawn beret. Her shoes were black and scuffed – perhaps hand-me-downs or purchased in the market. She sat down and took a pack of cigarettes from her handbag. He noticed that her hands were slightly trembling – from cold or fear he could not say.

"Hey you!" cried the bartender, a rough-looking man with a scar across his left cheek. "I can't afford women like you to come in and wait for customers without buying a drink. Either you buy or I'll throw you out. Times are too hard for non-paying customers."

The woman looked up, her face flushed.

"Of course, I'll go," she mumbled. Visibly flustered, she got up, wiping away a tear.

Fortescue went across and touched her arm. She bridled at his touch.

"Let me buy you a coffee."

"Thank you but that will not be necessary. He's right. I should go."

"I insist. It's snowing and you look cold. And I'm fed up reading about someone's travels in East Prussia long ago."

Before she could reply, he called for two coffees and beckoned her to his table. "You can't refuse me now."

He saw her hesitate as she resisted the temptation to walk out, then she unbuttoned her coat, revealing her slender figure, and sat beside him, glancing at him with tear-filled eyes.

The bartender placed the two mugs of coffee on the table.

"This is not a pick-up place, you know. I run a clean house – no prostitutes allowed."

"I'm clean, so is she," replied Fortescue. "Now bugger off."

The barman was taken aback. He was about to respond but thought better of it. Fortescue turned to the woman beside him.

"The coffee is undrinkable but, despite that regrettable fact, I suggest you drink it before it gets cold."

She said nothing as she took a sip.

"Are you from Munich?" he asked.

She looked at him briefly and then down at the mug cradled in her hands.

"Yes," she replied.

"Bad times?" he asked softly.

"Yes," she whispered. "And you? Where are you from? Your German is good but you're not from Germany."

"No, I'm not – just passing through."

"Oh," she murmured, "you're lucky. Are you American?"

"No. I'm English. I came here before the war and stayed with a German family, which improved my fluency. I had a good time – visiting art galleries and museums, and I met my first real girlfriend here. I even went to the opera across the road but didn't like the Wagner."

A faint smile crossed her face. "Me too."

"But recently I was in Nuremburg for the trial. I'm on my

way back to Berlin and then London. After that, I don't know what I'll do."

"Who did you stay with – when you were here before?"

"A family called Klaus. I went to find their house but it's gone. And what about you?" he asked.

"Nothing much to say," she replied, avoiding his eyes.

"You need to tell me a little more than that in exchange for the revelations about me."

She closed her eyes for a moment, her hands still tightly cradling the mug.

"I once had a family near here but like the family you looked for they're gone." She saw that he intended to press her further. "Please do not ask me any more questions. It was kind of you to buy me coffee but I don't know you and I have no wish to discuss the past. It's gone, beyond reach, and good riddance to it." She turned to look at him once again. "Please, no more questions," she repeated with a slight smile.

Fortescue looked at her. She was attractive, in her twenties he would guess. Her eyes were green and her lips delicate. There was only a trace of make-up. He had seen many women in uniform in Nuremburg but the young woman sitting beside him had a physical allure. He was struck by her long slim fingers curled around the mug. Looking at them gave him a sexual frisson. She suddenly pushed her chair back.

"Won't you have another coffee before you leave?" he asked.

"No. Thank you. I really must go."

"Go where?"

"I have a friend to see."

"Male or female?" he shot back.

"I said please stop asking me questions. I'm not in the witness box." She slid the mug across the table and stood up.

"I'm sorry for being so impertinent. Forgive me. I must stop the habit."

"You're forgiven, Mr Prosecutor," she said, half smiling.

"I was not a prosecutor. I got my bad habit from interrogating people, trying to find out why certain defendants did what they did. And I did not pull their fingernails out."

She sat down.

"And the result of your interrogations?" she asked.

"Here," he replied, pushing the stained copy of *Der Tagesspiegel* in front of her. She shuddered.

Again, she stood up.

"Thank you for the coffee. I must go now. I'm late."

"I have two opera tickets in my pocket – for tonight at the *Prinzregententheater* – a Mozart selection. Would you join me?"

"I can't. I'm doing something tonight."

"Are you? Or is that just an excuse?"

"Look, please stop asking questions!"

"Of course, I'm sorry. Look, here's one of the tickets. Take it. If you happen to be free later, join me. Let's end this drab day on a musical note. After all, while we listen to the music I can't ask you questions. The writer Aldous Huxley – you may have heard of him – once said, 'After silence, that which comes nearest to expressing the inexpressible is music.' We'll enjoy each other's silent company."

"It won't be possible," she insisted.

"Look, I won't take no for an answer." He thrust a ticket into her hand. "The performance starts at seven o'clock. I'll be there for sure. If you come, there will be a seat for you. If not, I will miss you."

She paused, looking at the ticket intently, then slowly put it in her handbag.

"Goodbye," she said.

He held out his hand. "By the way, my name is Richard Fortescue. In case you do me the pleasure of joining me this evening, may I ask your name?"

She looked at him. "Karin," she replied. She gave him a faint smile, her eyes still red from her earlier tears. She left the café without turning back.

He ordered another coffee and some bread and cheese. Would she come that evening or not? He doubted she would, but on the other hand she just might. If she did, he would be pleased to have an agreeable young woman next to him – an evening with the enemy, some of his colleagues might have said.

Half an hour later, Fortescue left the bar. He noticed on his way out a burly sullen-looking man trying to hide his face behind a crumpled newspaper but failing miserably to do so. He recognised the man from the day before – following him around the flea market. His superiors had warned him before leaving Nuremburg of ex-Nazis either seeking to escape from defeated Germany before they were arrested or anxious to settle old scores. And then there were the black-market entrepreneurs, eager to screw money out of the unsuspecting. Nor should he overlook the blackmailers making money out of those anxious to hide past crimes or misdemeanours under Allied occupation laws. Fortescue was under no illusion: he himself was probably under observation as an occupier, and buying *Mein Kampf* had been a breach of British army regulations. He would take all necessary care and remedial action if required to conceal what he had done.

Shortly before 7.00 p.m. he took his seat in the theatre – the second seat from the aisle in row F. After a short delay, the curtain rose at 7.10 p.m. A few minutes later, as the soprano sang *Ruhe sanft* from Mozart's *Zaide*, Karin slipped into the aisle seat beside him. He turned and briefly squeezed her arm. Her face showed no emotion.

After the performance, they walked out into the bitter cold. She still wore her green coat and beret. He noticed her shoes were different – high-heeled.

"Would you like something to eat?" he asked. "I'm sure we could find somewhere."

"No thank you. I had better go."

"Why is it better to go? You look cold. Perhaps we can find some warm soup somewhere."

"No, thank you. I really must leave."

"Why must you leave?" he asked.

"Because that's the way it is," she replied, her voice showing a trace of irritation.

"At least let me escort you home. The streets are unsafe this time of night."

"I would welcome that," she replied to his surprise.

He found a taxi. They went several blocks, stopping at a partially damaged tenement building not far from the *Hauptbahnhof*.

"On which floor do you live?"

"The third," she replied. "But I can find my way."

"I'll see you to the door."

Signalling the taxi driver to stay, Fortescue accompanied Karin to the bottom of the stairwell.

"I still don't know your surname."

"Eilers, Karin Eilers," she replied.

"Thank you."

He was sorely tempted to kiss her cheek but instead proffered his hand. She shook it gently and disappeared into the blackness. He stood in the stairwell listening to the click of her heels on the stone steps. Then he heard her voice.

"Leave me alone. I don't want to see you again. Please go away."

A muffled cry followed.

He ran up the dark stairs. In the flame of his lighter, he saw a dark hatted figure, collar turned up, pressing Karin against the wall, one gloved hand over her mouth and the other pulling up her coat and dress. She was struggling to escape her assailant's grip. The man spun round to receive Fortescue's fist in his face. He staggered back, clutching his nose. Fortescue pushed him to the floor, kicking him in the ribs. He grabbed hold of Karin.

"Come with me," he shouted, pulling her down the stairs behind him.

They scrambled into the taxi.

"Follow my directions," he instructed the driver. Periodically, he looked back to see whether they were being followed. There was no sign. He put his arm around Karin, who was struggling to hold back tears.

On arrival at the British safe house, he signed her in as a friend from his pre-war Munich visit. The concierge on the front door gave Fortescue a knowing look but made no comment. Once inside the small two-room apartment, she refused food but drank a large brandy. Her face was tear-stained and bruised, and two of her fingernails were broken from the struggle with her attacker. She gave an occasional sob. Resisting the urge to ask her questions, he gave her some aspirin and insisted that she take his bed. He would sleep on the sofa. He closed the bedroom door behind him.

He sat for a while thinking about what had happened and what he would do in the morning. Was she a prostitute who had failed to keep an appointment with a client, or did this striking well-spoken young woman have some other secret? Whatever the answer, it was evident she was at risk and he decided he would help her if she would let him. Despite the fact that he would be breaking the rules by fraternising with a German while on active duty, he would not abandon her. But how could he do that? In two days' time he was due to fly to Berlin. Could he possibly take her with him? Or could he defer his departure to find out more about her and find her a safe place to stay?

He threw some spare blankets on the sofa. Before going to sleep, he slowly opened the bedroom door. In the dim hall light, he saw she was awake, looking at him.

"I'm cold. And frightened."

He sat on the bed and took her hand. It was frozen.

"I'll get you another blanket. Like everywhere else, there's no heating."

"No, please just lie beside me. Put your arm around me. Make me feel safe and warm," she said, her eyes brimming with tears. "They will not leave me alone."

He decided not to ask who "they" were.

Without undressing, he did as she asked. She clasped his hand tightly, holding it against her chest. They fell asleep.

CHAPTER THREE

Return to Nuremburg

Fortescue woke early and slipped silently from the bed. Karin was still asleep, hardly moved from the position in which he had held her. After shaving and a shower, he went to the kitchen to reflect further on what to do. Being a Sunday morning, the street outside was empty, no sound apart from a distant church bell.

In his bed was a young woman he had picked up – there was no better description for what he had done – in a café the day before. He had persuaded her to go with him to the opera and then he had taken her to where she said she lived. He had punched and kicked a man who was trying to rape her, and brought her back to his billet. He had no idea who she was – apart from the name she had given him, and that she seemed to be German – or whether she was a prostitute or not. She was clearly frightened, but of what exactly he had no clue beyond a dark figure in a stairwell and a non-specific "they". Should he let her go after some breakfast or should he encourage her to stay so he could help her? But if he were to do that, he would need to ask her more questions – to find out more about her past. And if he were to do that, he would have to put her at ease. His billet was not the best place to do so. The other problem was that he was due to fly to Berlin the next day, to begin his journey home and possibly his eventual discharge from the army. He sipped another coffee, turning what had happened over and over in his mind. His head told him he should let her go but his heart said no; she seemed too vulnerable to abandon. But her vulnerability aside, there was a sexual magnetism about her.

He turned, suddenly aware that she was standing in the doorway looking at him, her arms clasped around her.

"Would you like some coffee?" he asked.

"Yes please," she replied, her face expressionless.

"And some breakfast?"

"No thank you."

"I think you should. I will cook you an army-style omelette."

She was about to say no but Fortescue put his finger to his lips.

"All right, Mr Interrogator, I will do as you say."

She ate silently, wrapped in his dressing gown. He watched her. At that moment, he decided to postpone his flight to Berlin and to encourage her to stay. He would be breaking the rules laid down by his superiors – about mixing with the local population – and being disloyal to Susannah. But to hell with it. This is what he wanted to do, even though at the back of his mind was the selfish motive of possible sexual gratification. He had not been to bed with a woman for over a year.

She looked up.

"Thank you for what you did last night. I don't know who he was. I frequently hear stories of young women in Berlin being raped by Russians but to experience it here in Munich is frightening. I will get dressed and leave you."

"Where will you go?"

"Back to my home – the one you saw last night, near the *Hauptbahnhof*," she replied.

"You can't go there. That place is unsafe. Stay here a day or so."

"No. I can't. That's where I live. Besides, my friend Frieda will be there."

He tried to dissuade her but she was set on leaving, agreeing, though, that he could accompany her.

*

An hour later they arrived at the tenement block by taxi. Insisting that he go with her upstairs, Fortescue asked the driver to wait. They climbed the stone staircase. On reaching the third floor, she pointed to the brown door on the right – flat number 7. He noticed that the door was ajar.

"Hello Frieda. It's Karin," she called out. She was about to push the door open when he stopped her.

"Stay back. Let me go first," he said firmly, pulling an army pistol from beneath his jacket. He entered a small, untidy hallway. She followed him. "Stay here, Karin. I think something may have happened." He nudged open the door in front of him.

The room was cheaply furnished – what you might find in a brothel: worn, stained, gaudy furnishings. Then he noticed the body in the corner, half covered by a threadbare carpet. He pulled it back. It was a young blond woman, naked, her hands bound, her mouth gagged. There was congealed blood on the floor. Her throat had been cut and across her chest had been incised the words, *Heil Hitler!* He heard a movement behind him. Spinning round he saw Karin crumple to her knees, her face white with terror. After helping her to a chair and urging her to put her head between her legs, he covered the body with a shawl that had been slung across an armchair. Hearing a faint sound, he turned towards a half-open door. He pushed it slowly, his pistol cocked. Hanging from a hook in the ceiling beam was the body of a man, swinging slightly. The body was naked apart from a blood-stained German army cap on his head. The victim's hands were tied behind his back and his mouth stuffed with paper. Around his neck hung a piece of cardboard on which had been scrawled in blood, *I am a coward.*

He heard Karin next door retching. He grabbed her by the arm but she struggled to escape his grip.

"What have they done to Gerhard? I must see. Let me go to him. He's my brother!"

Breaking free, she went into the room. Fortescue put his arms around her, holding her tightly to him.

"We must go now. There's nothing you can do for him – for either of them – and this is not a place where either of us should be. I will call the police but let's get out of here first."

"But I need some clothes."

"No, you don't. This is a crime scene. We'll find you clothes elsewhere."

Karin again broke free from his grip.

"I must find it. I must find it," she insisted.

"Find what?"

"The book – I have to find the book!"

"Which book?" he asked with rising impatience.

"The book, it is here somewhere. I must find it. For God's sake, where did they hide it?"

"Who are 'they'?"

"Frieda and Schatzi!" she shouted. She crawled about the floor, crying. "I remember. They put it in here." She tore at a floorboard near Frieda's body and put her hand into the cavity beneath. "It must be here. It must be here."

He knelt beside her. Pushing her aside, he put his own hand into the cavity, reaching as far as he could. After a few seconds, he pulled out a small black book – a notebook.

"That's it. That's it."

She snatched hold of it and stuffed it into her handbag.

"Now, Karin, for God's sake, we've got to get out of here."

The taxi took them back to his billet.

Her face was deathly white. Once again he administered aspirin and insisted that she lie down. He called Max Steiner on the phone.

"Max, I've had a tip-off that there are two bodies in an apartment block near the main station. They appear to have been murdered by Nazis. Please inform the local police and let your boys know too."

"How do you know this?"

"I can't say. My source is anonymous but credible."

"I didn't know you had sources in Munich."

"You would be surprised by my sources – in the British tradition of high-quality wartime intelligence."

"When can we have our farewell drink together? You're going to Berlin tomorrow, yes?"

"No, I'm not. I'm about to call Logistics to say I want a few more days in Munich."

"Why do you want to do that? You told me that you wanted to get back into Susannah's arms as quickly as possible."

"I do, Max, I do. But I have a piece of unfinished business to complete."

"Can I help?"

"No, you can't. It's personal."

"Don't tell me you're having a fling with a German girl?"

"No, Max. It's about a girl but there's no fling. I'll catch up with you in Berlin when I pass through. I promise."

"OK. Make sure you keep your promise. And bring me a picture of the girl."

"I'll see what I can do."

Karin was asleep. He wanted her to stay. If she did, his first task would be to comfort her and he'd do his best. But, accomplished interrogator that he was, he was curious to find out more about her. At present, she was little more than a passer-by – someone he had met the day before in a café and who had accompanied him to the opera. Within the space of twelve hours, someone had tried to rape her and her friends were dead – murdered. Who exactly was this young woman? Why had her friends been murdered? Did she have any idea who might have killed them? The flat he had seen was a brothel. She had told him she lived there. That would suggest she was indeed a prostitute. And then there was the black notebook she had been desperate to find. So many questions he could ask but not now – he did not want to drive away a woman to whom he felt attracted. He had to find the right circumstances, the right place, to put her at ease – break down her guard – and to get to know her better. But where, that was the question.

He broke the news to Logistics that he would not be at the airbase in the morning.

It was late afternoon when she awoke, her face tear-streaked and still white. Her eyes lacked focus.

"Karin, tonight you will stay here. You will be safe. But in the meantime you need fresh clothes. I have a British military contact here – Dorothy Maddox. She helps to look after us personnel in transit. She will take you shortly to a shop to get some – a couple of dresses, a coat, shoes. She knows where to go. I won't be far away, to ensure nothing happens to you. Tomorrow, we are going out of town for the day so we can talk."

"But I have no money to buy clothes."

"I've given Mrs Maddox some money."

"I won't let you do this. I'm not a client of yours, a recipient of your favours in return for sleeping with you."

"Karin, listen. You will stay here and moreover you will go with Mrs Maddox because you have no other option. Last night, in the flat where you said you lived, your friend Frieda was brutally murdered and your brother hanged – possibly by former Nazis. Their motive is unclear to me. Perhaps it was because they believed they had been betrayed or could not find what they were looking for. Perhaps you know the reason. Maybe it has something to do with the black book you took away. But now is not the time to talk about it. Karin, just do as I say – and that's an order. I like you and I don't want anything to happen to you. Is that understood?"

She nodded. He went to put his arm around her, but she shrugged him away.

Later, accompanied by Dorothy, Karin returned with three parcels. While he and Dorothy prepared a simple meal and talked, she changed. She reappeared in a soft-red fitted dress with a blue velvet collar and cuffs. Its nipped-in waist was accentuated by a narrow velvet band with a small bow to one side. She wore high-heeled shoes. Her shoulder-length hair was partially pinned back and she had applied some make-up which his generosity had also bought. Her face was still pale and her hand trembled as she accepted a glass of wine from Dorothy. Conversation over their modest supper was about incidental matters, with he and Dorothy doing most of the talking. She joined in from time to time, in between her frequent cigarettes.

After Dorothy had left, Fortescue and Karin sat opposite each other at the kitchen table. The candle stuck in the old wine bottle between them was fast near extinction.

"Tomorrow, at Mrs Maddox's suggestion, I've arranged for us to go to Würmsee. I went there before the war. A contact of hers will take us out on the lake in his boat – a covered one, I hasten to say. Then you can tell me more about Karin Eilers and your black book."

She looked at him in a hostile way.

"What if I don't want to go, Mr Fortescue? What if I have nothing to say, Mr Interrogator?"

"If you wish to be formal, so will I. Fräulein Eilers, it is my supposition that, in all probability, had I not been with you last night, you would now be dead – your throat possibly cut like Frieda's. Someone wanted her, Gerhard and you killed. I don't know why. At Nuremburg, we convicted the leaders of the Reich and more of their henchmen will follow in their footsteps to the noose or imprisonment. But there are hundreds of others whose hands are steeped in blood, who have yet to answer for their crimes. Maybe it was some of them who killed Frieda and your brother. If you have any information to add to what we know about a regime that dragged this country into the abyss, it is important that you tell me. Don't withhold it. Do you understand? It's what you have to do."

"Is that the reason why you bought me clothes? To help me become a compliant witness – a tactic I am told a sophisticated interrogator pursues – or is it because you wish to make me more presentable, to suit your taste in women?" she replied caustically.

"How wrong you are!"

"Am I?" she answered. "I know enough about the motives of men."

"Listen to me. I did not give Mrs Maddox money in order to bribe you to sleep with me. I did it to help you put the past behind you. Besides, you needed fresh clothes – not clothes from an apartment reeking of death. And by the way, the dress suits you."

"Are you making a pass at me?" she enquired, gently placing her hands on the table.

"Certainly not," he countered.

"You're good at words but is not the real truth that you want to dress me like this so I become your live doll to play with?"

"That's absurd!"

"Is it? Is it not the case that by dressing me in clothes you've bought for me, you feel you have acquired the proprietorial right to undress me and fuck me at pleasure?"

"I know you are still distressed by what you saw this morning. But don't be so bloody cynical. I'm not making a pass at you – though if you really want to know I do find you attractive."

She sat back and lit a cigarette, her palpable inner rage appearing to subside. He tried to anticipate her next move.

"I'm a prostitute – not out of choice but because Frieda and I had to offer sex to survive. I'm dirty – untouchable, some might say. You probably guessed that and want to hide the fact by buying me clothes."

He looked at her. She was seeking to provoke him.

"You are not untouchable," he replied.

He placed his hands on the table, moving his fingertips slowly towards her. She responded, returning her own to the tabletop and edging them ever closer. Their fingertips touched, provoking a mutual spark. Neither spoke, the contact still unbroken.

"Shall we put out the candle and go to bed?" he asked.

"I'm nothing. I'm worthless," she whispered.

"No, you're not."

Their fingers locked.

"Shall we go to bed?" he asked again.

"That is the first time I've ever been asked," she said, barely audible.

Tears welled in her eyes. She nodded. He snuffed out the candle.

In bed, she pulled him ever more deeply into her. When she came, she uttered a great cry – not of pleasure but as though she had exorcised some evil spirit. She fell asleep, her body cradled in the arc of his and her arms pinning his across her breasts. He lay awake, concluding that he had reached a fork in the road and chosen a path that would take him through thick dark woods ahead. He had to stay composed. Tomorrow the interrogation would begin.

*

They left early the next morning for Würmsee. He had dressed in mufti, rather than his uniform, as being more appropriate to the occasion. Since waking they had said little to one another and equally little was said in the taxi; as throughout their earlier conversations, they spoke in German. At Starnberg, on the north shore of the lake, they went immediately to the jetty, where a small dilapidated wooden vessel was moored.

"Are you Herr Bauer?" Fortescue asked.

"Yes," replied the old man, his face half concealed by a thick grey beard and a stained blue cap pulled over his eyes.

"Good. My friend and I would like to go to Seeshaupt."

"I know. At your service," Bauer replied.

They boarded the boat, followed by an elderly couple and two middle-aged women with baskets. At the last moment, a man in his forties stepped aboard, the collar of his thick black coat turned up and his fedora tipped well down. After a brief wait, while Bauer gave his passengers blankets to keep them warm – despite the closed sides to the boat and the tarpaulin across the deck, it would be a cold and damp journey, he warned – he cast off and the boat slipped its mooring.

Linking her arm in his, Karin asked Fortescue in a whisper when the interrogation would begin, in a manner that suggested she looked forward to playing a game.

"Not now," he answered, pointing at the man sitting one row up on the other side of the deck. "It will come – later."

The boat chugged slowly across the lake, its dark waters concealing the secrets of its depths.

Some two hours later, after several stops, the boat docked at the small town of Seeshaupt.

"Could you collect us tomorrow, to take us back to Starnberg?" Fortescue asked Bauer.

"There's not much here to see but, yes, if that's what you want. I'll be back for sure."

"Thank you," said Fortescue. He thrust some dollars into the old man's hands. "I'll double it if you really do return."

"I will," replied Bauer. "It's always a pleasure doing business with an Englishman, even though you beat us twice in war."

He and Fortescue smiled at each other.

21

Karin and Fortescue walked around the small deserted town, still her arm in his. He was soon aware that they were being followed. As they turned a corner, he looked back. It was the man from the boat. Was he following the woman on his arm or was he following him? If him, was he a friend or foe? He touched the left side of his overcoat to make sure his pistol was still there. Retracing their steps, they played a trick on the man following them. The pursuer became the pursued. Back at the waterfront they passed a hotel with a *Closed* sign in the door. Disregarding it, Fortescue and Karin went inside. A bell rang as they closed the door behind them. A sour-faced woman came to the reception desk.

"We're closed," she said gruffly.

"We can see that you are. But as we've missed the boat back to Starnberg, we would like to spend the night here. I will pay well – in dollars."

"I'll get the proprietor, Herr Steckler. He's my husband."

The proprietor came to the desk and glimpsing the US dollars he instantly agreed.

"My friend and I have much to discuss as we have not seen much of each other in the past year or so. We would like something to eat and drink and to sit in front of a fire and talk."

"And I assume you would like a comfortable bed too," interrupted Steckler with a twinkle in his eye. "Such a striking companion you have. Is she your wife?"

"No," replied Fortescue. "We're just getting to know each other better."

"My wife and I will be happy to oblige you young lovers," said Herr Steckler, beaming.

That evening, Fortescue and Karin sat either side of a large log fire, the wood hissing as it caught. A half-empty bottle of wine stood on a low table between them next to a candle burning in a heavy brass stick.

"So, Fräulein Karin Eilers, who are you?" Thus began the interrogation.

As he waited for her reply, he studied her face in the flickering shadows of the fire. She had high cheekbones and finely drawn lips. Her skin was like porcelain. Her green eyes, piercing, constantly probing, the lashes emphasised by mascara, were almond-shaped beneath strong eyebrows. Her shoulder-length hair was pinned back in the fashion she had worn it the night before. Her lipstick was dark red – perhaps too dark, he thought. He observed how she crossed her long slender legs without her delicate hands pulling down the hem of her dress. The vulnerability and anger he had seen the previous night had disappeared, or perhaps it was hidden behind a mask of insouciance. The clock in the room ticked; a murmur of wind outside; the fire crackled as he threw on another log. Shedding her high heels, she tucked her legs beneath her and took a long draw on her cigarette. She gave the impression of self-confidence in the task he had set her.

"My name is Karin Eilers. I was born in Kreuzberg in Berlin in 1921."

As she began to tell her story, he took a small black notebook and a short stub of pencil from his pocket. She stopped.

"Is this a formal interrogation with a typed record at the end that I will be obliged to sign, leading to my indictment?" Though she was smiling, there was an icy tone to her words.

"No, there will be no indictment – only a statement of the truth to me so I can ensure your protection," he replied in a matter-of-fact manner. If she wished to play a game, so would he.

"Is your wish to protect me – based on your record of what I divulge – designed to give you a hold over me? Is it a means to make me your mistress, locking me in an unwilling relationship only you can end whenever you choose?"

She was still smiling, but her words dripped with cynicism – possibly, he thought, reflecting what she had endured as a prostitute.

"Karin, listen to me. Don't refight the battle we had last night. Outside in Seeshaupt, in Munich, in Berlin and elsewhere is a world of chancers, purveyors of revenge, the morally corrupt, the cynical and most of all those guilty of unimaginable crimes, as retold at Nuremburg. Regrettably, the end of the war will not end corruption, betrayal and ambition achieved at the cost of others because the human race is tainted, just as Germany – the land that on the one hand produced Bach and his sublime music in an age of reason and that on the other created Auschwitz and Sachsenhausen, used by a regime to dispense horror and cruelty – is tainted."

She turned away to look at the fire.

"Two nights ago, someone wanted you dead – either a deluded Nazi sympathiser or someone seeking revenge on Nazi sympathisers. I've yet to hear who you think it was. But whoever he was he wanted to rape you and then probably slit your throat. Maybe the black book you removed had something to do with it. I like you. You are attractive and I enjoyed sleeping with you last night. But that pleasure aside, I want to help you – that is all."

He looked at her. She turned to face him. He thought her mask had slipped and for a moment or two he saw the vulnerability he had glimpsed the night before. But if it had it was soon in place again.

"Of course, you're right. What I said was unjustified – words from an embittered young woman."

She took a sip of wine, her hand trembling for a second as she did so. Then, lighting another cigarette, she continued.

"My father, Stefan, a Berliner, was a printer by trade – a good one by all accounts – running his own small business. My mother, Helga, was a teacher – a glamorous Bavarian. In 1930, my father, finding it harder to keep the business going, joined the National Socialists, attracted by their message of national renewal. He became a Brownshirt, rapidly rising up through the ranks and using his printing press to produce some of their propaganda. He was killed in Hitler's putsch against Röhm. He shouldn't have died but unfortunately he got in the way of the SS that terrible night. Surprisingly, my mother showed little grief. She soon lost interest in teaching and was sacked one day for insubordination. She found it hard to get other work, so as a family we struggled for a while. To earn extra money, she slept with a few men and through a particular liaison met someone who got her a menial job in the Information Ministry. Soon she joined the Party and before long became involved with the Party newspaper – the *Völkischer Beobachter*. In due course, she caught the eye of Goebbels. He sent her back to Munich. So, at the age of seventeen – in 1938 – I concluded my education in Bavaria at a smart school full of posh Nazi children. My mother went sometimes to the Berghof. She loved being in that crowd there – on the fringe of the close circle around Hitler, imitating the style and manners of the glittering women who clustered around the man they all idolised. My mother seemed to have no difficulty over money at that time. I don't know where she got it from. But she used it to buy good clothes and we never went without. When the war started, my mother was transferred back to Berlin as part of the circle around Goebbels. I stayed behind in Munich. After a brief spell at a Party 'finishing school' – for ideology rather than manners, as you can imagine – I became a secretary in a small company."

"And what was Gerhard doing?" asked Fortescue.

"Gerhard was three years older than me. He had done well at school but afterwards he drifted. He did various jobs which paid little. Then he met some people in the army and decided to join up. I remember the day he came home, proudly showing us his military *Ausweis*, and how young and innocent he looked in the ID-card photo. In the spring of 1939 his unit was one of those that moved into what was left of Czechoslovakia and he wrote to say he had witnessed Hitler's proclamation of the Protectorate of Bohemia and Moravia. Then later he was sent to the Eastern Front which he abhorred – too close, he said, to the special *Einsatzgruppen* tasked with liquidating all undesirables. He stayed in the army but, like many others, deserted at the end of the war and somehow managed to get to Munich. I was at Frieda's by then. She took him in, too."

"After the war ended, what did he do?" asked Fortescue.

"Not much," Karin replied. "He largely stayed at home or did odd jobs for people. He was good with his hands."

"Did he have many friends?"

"Few, I would say."

"Did he have any girlfriends?"

"Only one, as I recall. She was a shy girl – Bavarian, judging by her accent. But I think he preferred being with men."

"Can you remember her name?"

"Clotilde, if I recall correctly. One day they had an argument and we never saw or heard of her again. It upset Gerhard for a while. He barely went out. If he did, it was with a couple of men. I think they were homosexuals."

Karin sipped her wine.

"What next?" Fortescue asked.

"What do you mean, 'what next'?"

"I want to hear the rest of your story. What happened to you in Munich?"

She became irritated.

"Look, Mr Interrogator, you don't own me. You never will. So, stop telling me what to do, what to say."

"I'm not telling you what to say. I'm asking you – politely – to tell me the rest of your story. How many times do I have to tell you – I want to help you."

"Too many people have tried to tie me down. I tell everyone that if they do I won't stay."

"Karin, I'm not trying to tie you down. I'm not telling you what to do. Believe me."

He filled her wine glass and lit a cigarette, placing it between her lips. They sat silently for a while.

"Then I met Frieda. She was two years older than me – an extrovert who dressed expensively and well. After a while, she invited me to join her in her apartment. I readily agreed. There was little money coming from my mother in Berlin and my secretarial job had become precarious. It was soon apparent that there was a price to pay at Frieda's. She was a high-class prostitute. Often senior Nazis in uniform would come to the flat for drinks and sex. Initially, I just helped serve drinks but before long I performed my first sexual favour. I hated it but as the hardship of war got worse the comforts of life became scarcer and more expensive. So, I reluctantly became more involved – joining Frieda in bed with senior Nazis performing rituals beneath a swastika flag draped over the bedhead. She loved putting on their jackets and caps. I think it gave her a thrill. On a few occasions, Frieda and I were invited to some of the houses – or billets, I suppose – in the grounds of the Berghof. She once introduced me to Hermann Fegelein, the SS *Gruppenführer*. I disliked him – particularly after I saw how roughly he treated Frieda one evening when he was drunk. One day we even went up to the Eagle's Nest. Hitler wasn't there but we met Eva Braun who took us out on the veranda to look at the mountains across the valley. But as the war began to go badly we slowly fell out of favour with Frieda's clients and we started to get the riff-raff instead. Knowing how much I disliked having sex with these thugs, Frieda tried her best to shield me from the more extreme men. Despite the hardship and occasional violence meted out to her – and I sometimes wondered if she succumbed too readily to the treatment she received – Frieda remained in high spirits, even when we fell on yet harder times. And for that I admired her even more, not least because she taught me a great deal about men, their cruelty and betrayal, and tricks of the trade to avoid the worst physical violence. Thankfully, I avoided too many bruises. You, Mr Interrogator, are a gentle sex partner. But perhaps that is part of your training in the subtler art of questioning."

"Thank you for the compliment," he replied.

She stubbed out her cigarette, nonchalantly threw the butt into the fire and lit up another.

"I went to Berlin for a while during that time, to my mother's, but she seemed even more dazzled by the Party than before, committed to its work. I scarcely saw her, which was perhaps just as well. And with the bombing … Life with Frieda, however hard, seemed preferable and I returned to Munich. Then one evening, after you and the Americans had landed in France, a senior member of the SS – Frieda called him by a pet name, Schatzi, though I never understood why – came to see us. He confessed that the war was going badly. The future was bleak but it was important that certain information was preserved, in case it might be useful later if the regime's help was ever sought in a last-minute coalition against the Reds. Frieda agreed and on receipt of some cash undertook to store two locked tin boxes of papers. Schatzi put them in a cupboard hidden behind a wardrobe. From time to time he came with some small bundles of loose papers which he put in the tins. On his last ever visit, when Berlin was becoming encircled by the Russians, he brought the black book. He said it was a precious commodity, which must never fall into the wrong hands. As he was in a rush he asked Frieda to hide it with the other papers, rather than doing it himself. She told him that as the wardrobe was too heavy for us to move she would hide it under the floorboards in her sitting room instead, where she kept some money for an emergency. She showed him where. He nodded his approval and quickly left as the siren began to warn of another enemy air raid. We never saw him again but occasionally we would receive messages – from whom was not clear – written on scraps of paper, insisting that we remain vigilant of what was in our care as it might be required for the conduct of certain important business after the Reich's defeat. When the war finally ended, Frieda spoke of her, Gerhard and me leaving Munich to find some peace and quiet – to end our dependence on prostitution. But it never happened. The rest you know."

"What happened to your mother?" Fortescue asked.

"In late 1944, I received a written message from her. She was still in Berlin. The bombing was bad, she said, but the Führer would prevail as he had always done. That was the last I heard of her. I have no idea whether she is alive or dead. I am all that is left and at the age of twenty-five I have little to show in achievement – except a good knowledge of the anatomy of men, what the crueller sort do to achieve sexual gratification, regardless of the pain it might cause women, and, of course, surviving."

He asked her some other questions but her answers added little more information that could possibly be of use. Whether her story was true in every respect he could not say.

"Have you finished?" she asked him, as he put his notebook down and lit two cigarettes, one of which he gave to her. She slowly stretched her legs before crossing them, giving him a sexual thrill as she did so, which perhaps was what she intended.

"Yes. I have. We'll discuss the notebook later once you've allowed me to see it."

"I will – in the morning," she replied.

He placed some more wood on the fire.

"Do you dance?" he asked.

"Yes," she replied, "but not for a long time."

He went across to the sideboard on which rested a wind-up gramophone. Beside it was a pile of records in tattered covers. He flicked through them. There was no jazz or swing but he noticed a recording of Beethoven's *Romance No. 2*. He had seen Yehudi Menuhin perform it at the Wigmore Hall in London, shortly before leaving for Germany in 1938. Its lyricism and cadences had moved him so much that he had bought a recording to give to Susannah on her birthday.

Fortescue put the record on the gramophone, wound it up and placed the stylus on the spinning disc. As the music began, he turned to Karin.

"This is not music to which one usually dances but it's music to which we can take some gentle steps together."

He beckoned her. Slipping on her shoes and throwing her cigarette in the fire, she placed her hand in his. Putting his arm around her waist, he pressed her tightly against him. She did not resist. Barely moving and her head on his shoulder they swayed to the violinist's lilting melody.

"Thank you, Richard, for your protection and your affection. I wish this moment would last but you and I know it won't."

It was the first time she had called him by his first name.

"Karin, don't let words or time spoil the magic."

He kissed her. She put her arms around his neck and returned his kiss gently. He placed his hands on her hips, pressing her thighs close against his. They continued to sway slowly to the melody, each locked in private thoughts. For him, she was magnetic, beguiling and enigmatic. He was not sure he had reached the truth of her story. He would probe further. But for the moment he wanted to put that task – and the risks he was taking – aside. They kissed yet again and, when the music ended, went to bed – as playful lovers.

He woke early; she still asleep.

He sat by the window looking at her. Though not beautiful, she conveyed a strong allure that had captivated him from the moment she sat beside him in the café. She was the perfect softly spoken foil to his panache and playfulness, qualities that Susannah said had played their part in kindling her love for him. In bed, Karin had discarded her abrasive shield to reveal vulnerability, genuine rather than contrived. She had been mischievous as they engaged, easily aroused but each tactile move had been on her terms – like a cat toying with a skein of wool – one moment the pleasure of physical connection, another moment teasing denial. Whether her confident sexual skill, which he thought could easily descend into something darker, had been acquired from meeting the varied tastes of past clients or was a genuine expression of sexual feeling towards him, he could not judge.

She turned but did not wake. She had admitted she had been a prostitute who slept with the like of those who had been his enemy at Nuremburg. Had she done so for pleasure or self-preservation? He had left Nuremburg with quiet pride that he had played a small part in punishing evil. For two nights, he had slept with a woman whose body had been enjoyed by SS officers who perhaps had committed unspeakable crimes, cruelty and depravity. Should that not repel him? Had he not compromised his principles for momentary pleasure? Or should he dismiss the thought he had betrayed them and surrender to the physical satisfaction she provided? Was it the case that his spirit was willing but his flesh weak? The deed was done. He was increasingly attracted to her, not repelled by her past association. His conscience was clear.

He noticed that her handbag was open. He peered inside and saw the black notebook. Again she stirred. He eased the book from its concealment. The cover bore a silver imprint of the SS symbol. Beneath it were the words *Most Secret*. On the inside title page was written, in thick black ink:

Information Gathered for the Attention of Reichsführer Himmler

He silently turned a few of the pages. They appeared to contain a list of tightly written entries in some form of code. Each entry was in a format that might suggest names and other details. The code format was vaguely reminiscent of one he had seen in a document that passed across his desk in Nuremburg early in his assignment. He would need to return there to see if he could find the document and use it to try to decipher the entries.

She began to wake. He deftly slid the book back into her handbag. What had the book to do with her and the bodies in her flat? Where had it come from? Who wanted it? What exactly was the information it contained? Had Karin told him the whole truth or was she playing a game? She had answered some of his questions but there were so many more. And if he went back to Nuremburg, what would happen to her? Might another killer seek her out? And if she went into hiding, might he lose contact with her?

She woke. He bent over her and kissed her gently. She drew him down, insisting they make love again. His questions would have to wait.

After breakfast, they went for a long walk, hand in hand, in the woods above Seeshaupt. Fortescue was soon aware that they were being followed. They doubled back and approached their shadow from behind.

"Who are you?" asked Fortescue.

The man, whom he had not seen before, spun round.

"I want her," he snarled in reply.

"She's not for the taking," answered Fortescue.

"But she is," said the man. "She is one of us. She belongs to us – just like the others. And I will have her."

He pulled a pistol from his coat pocket and took aim. But Fortescue was the faster with his. Their assailant fell to the ground, Fortescue's gunshot echoing through the trees. Karin gasped. Fortescue bent down. Though there was no obvious bullet wound, the man lay motionless. He quickly rifled through the man's pockets but found nothing other than a slim black wallet containing a few Reichsmarks. There was no identity card. He put the wallet back and kicked some leaves over the body.

"We must go," he said, already hurrying away, pulling Karin behind him.

They returned to the hotel, paid the bill and sat on the

quayside waiting for the boat to reappear, as it did – on time. As they boarded, Fortescue saw a police vehicle threading its way up the road above the village towards the woods.

Neither spoke on the way back to Munich. That night, in his billet, they talked into the small hours. She fell asleep on the sofa, wrapped in a blanket. He sat at the table and opened his notebook to record what had happened over the past few days – not his thoughts, just the brief facts. He looked at her and then at the embers in the grate. He had blood on his hands. Though he and Karin might have been seen returning from the woods at Seeshaupt, he was not deterred. As a trained interrogator, he knew what to say under pressure, how to throw an opponent off the scent. He would go to Nuremburg, and she with him, to try to find the document he had seen with the code similar to that in the black book in her handbag. But if he were to become a marked man hunted by accomplices of the man he had killed, then she was a marked woman – sought by unknown assailants for what she possessed. Moreover, according to newspaper reports, the city police wished the assistance of a young woman, known only as K, in connection with the discovery of two murdered people with whom she was believed to have lived in a flat near the *Hauptbahnhof*. They were now on the run. To complicate matters, he was even more physically attracted to her. Indeed, was he possibly falling in love with her? He had broken all the military rules to which he was subject. She stirred.

"Richard, come."

He did not resist.

"Who owns whom?" he whispered as they lay together.

"That remains to be seen," she replied.

He woke early, as was his habit, and phoned Max. He needed his help. They met in a dingy café near the *Hauptbahnhof*.

"I have to go back to Nuremburg. I need to check something. I won't be long. While I'm gone I want you to do me a favour."

"Why the hell do you want to go back there? Our job is done. They're packing up. You've got Susannah waiting for you in London and I've got a girl waiting in Berlin. I don't understand, Rich."

Fortescue hated being called Rich but now was not the time to pick a fight about it.

"Level with me, Rich. What's this all about? And, more to the point, what's the favour?"

"I've met a girl. Karin. She may have the key to important information about what happened to some Nazis who have disappeared."

"She's not by any chance the girl the police are looking for?"

"Yes, she is," replied Fortescue. "Whoever murdered the two in the flat nearly got her as well but she managed to escape – with my help. I would like you to take her to Berlin and put her in a safe place where she can wait for me and the answers I hope to find in Nuremburg."

Max was momentarily lost for words.

"You must be joking, Rich."

"I'm not, Max. I once did you a big favour. I want this favour in return."

"Are you sleeping with her?" Max asked.

"Yes," came the curt reply.

"Who's the dominant partner – she or you?"

"We're equal. But it's not about sex. It's about making her safe, giving her a new future. Then I can return to London and Susannah."

"Really, Rich, is life that simple, that neat? Or are you bullshitting me? You want me to take this girl to Berlin – a girl the Munich cops are keen to interview about a double murder, a girl who may be mixed up with ex-Nazis – and place my career on the line?"

"Yes, Max, that is exactly what I'm asking you to do – just that and nothing more. Remember, Max, how I covered for you when you passed a piece of unauthorised classified information to the Russians in return for the compromising picture they had of you in bed with that brunette from their field security? I gave you a story that got you off the hook. As I've said, it's payback time."

Max's face flushed.

"OK, Rich. I will, just this one time. Then we're quits. Do you understand?"

Fortescue nodded. "It's a deal."

He returned to his billet and broke the news to Karin.

"I don't want to go to Berlin. I hate Americans."

"Why do you hate Americans?"

"I just do," she replied.

He knew there was more to it than that.

"Look, Karin, I don't give a damn what you think about Americans. Either you do as I say or you can walk out the door. We've been followed since our return from Würmsee. There is a man standing across the road watching this building. Go and look for yourself. If you leave, which you can do, chances are you'll either be picked up by the police or you'll be kidnapped by those seeking you, the notebook and whatever else. I'm giving you this choice because I care about you. I like you. I enjoy your company. I enjoy being in bed with you. So, what's your decision? Go or stay? Time is of the essence."

She went to the window and saw the man across the street – hatted and with upturned collar. She turned to look at Fortescue. He tried to read the thoughts behind her anxious green eyes. She had been so badly burned by men – all those filthy Nazis who had forced themselves between her thighs. She had escaped lightly, unlike her friend Frieda. In front of her was a British army officer, who was expert at seeking the truth in an almost clinical way. And he had been a gentle lover in bed. He was offering her a way out. She moved towards him, flicking her hair back – an action he liked, as she undoubtedly knew.

"I'll stay," she whispered. "I'll do as you ask. But don't leave me alone in Berlin too long. I will miss you. I want you with me in bed."

She placed her arms around his neck and gently kissed him. He put his arms around her waist.

"Thank you, Karin. I will get to Berlin as quickly as I can."

Later that day, Max came in uniform to the billet. After a few minutes, he and Fortescue, also in uniform, emerged gripping Karin by her arms between them. They got into a US army jeep and left for the airbase.

Early the next morning, she said goodbye to Fortescue and then, with Max, boarded the military aircraft for Berlin. He returned to Munich to seek Dorothy's help in getting to Nuremburg as quickly as possible. In his greatcoat pocket was the black book. He was now up to his neck in trouble, as he had already confessed to Dorothy Maddox.

As he left the following morning by road for Nuremburg, he received two messages from Dorothy. The first was from Max to say that his flight companion was now under surveillance in a safe house in Berlin. The other was from Susannah to say that her father, General Thomas, had managed to make tentative arrangements for her to fly with him to Berlin. Their reunion would not have to wait until London.

CHAPTER FOUR

The Nave with No Roof

Travelling once again by road, Fortescue counted each slow mile in his impatience to reach the war-shattered city of Nuremburg, about which he had read extensively before joining the tribunal.

Long ago it had been one of the famed cities of the Holy Roman Empire, an imperial treasure chest. Its celebrated son, Albrecht Dürer, had epitomised medieval Germany. Later, Richard Wagner's opera *The Mastersingers of Nuremburg* had constituted another of its cultural peaks. Then in the 1930s had come the infamous Nazi Party rallies and most despicable of all the Nuremburg Laws, first declared at the 1935 rally which Leni Riefenstahl – the German director, producer, screenwriter, photographer and propagandist for the Nazis – had filmed. He had watched the film one evening not long after arriving in the city. The laws had excluded all Jews from Reich citizenship and had prohibited them from marrying or having sexual relationships with persons of German or related blood. Now, in 1946, Nuremburg – including its medieval core – still lay in ruins from Allied bombing. Just as in Munich and Berlin, people went about their daily business in silence and without expression, as they and the city tried to forget the past and face a new and uncertain future. Within an hour or so of his arrival, he wanted to leave as quickly as he could – to put behind him the smell of death that still seemed to hang over everything. He wanted to get to Berlin and see Karin before the likely arrival of Susannah.

He was not surprised that so few of his colleagues and friends remained at the court building where he had spent so many months. Not only had most of the people gone but so had the bulk of the court documents – mainly to the United States. He asked the few colleagues who were left whether he could look at some of the remaining boxes still awaiting shipment. His request aroused some curiosity, not least because he was back in Nuremburg so soon after saying it was necessary for him to get to Berlin without further delay and from there to London. He explained that there were one or two loose ends he had to tie up. Those who knew him for his earlier diligence did not question his motive.

He spent all the following morning perusing the documentation that had not yet been despatched, looking for the item he remembered, but by the early afternoon it was evident his search was fruitless. He would have to look elsewhere, wherever that might be.

In the early evening, he arranged to meet Bob Pritchett, a burly Metropolitan Police sergeant, easy-going but shrewd, who had been part of the security personnel guarding the British prosecution team. They met in a bar on the edge of the old town. They talked about the latest news from London and recalled some old wartime drinking haunts in the backstreets of Westminster and Soho.

"It's good to see you, Richard, but why on earth are you back here? Your work finished weeks ago. You said goodbye and told us you were looking forward to getting Susannah back in your arms. Now, suddenly you're here, leafing through what little is left of the court documentation. We all knew the Americans wouldn't waste any time in shipping everything back to the States. So, why did you bother?"

"I just had to check something out. But I couldn't find what I wanted."

"There was always something secretive about you. Knowing you, you're on to something. Maybe our intelligence people have already signed you up."

"No, they haven't. And I wouldn't touch them, even if they asked me. The fact is I came across a few scraps of information in Munich and I wanted to check them out against an SS document I had seen during the preparation for the trial. I came on the off chance that the cross-reference might still be here but I was unlucky. The Americans moved even faster than I thought."

"So, a wasted trip?" replied Pritchett.

"It would seem so," answered Fortescue, ordering them another beer.

"What were you trying to check?" enquired Pritchett.

"I can't say because I'm not sure what exactly I'm looking for."

"Can't or won't say?" countered Pritchett.

"The former, not the latter," replied Fortescue, becoming uncomfortable at Pritchett's perceptive questions.

"You obviously think it's important enough to delay your departure from Germany."

"You know what it's like – something nags at your mind."

Pritchett looked at him, unconvinced.

"Whatever you're up to, be careful, Richard. We don't have many friends in these parts."

"Why do you say that?" asked Fortescue.

"This country is broken. Life is hard. This city, like other places in this defeated nation, has many people with a past to hide, a score to settle or those looking for information to sell. You and I and the rest of us are rich pickings. We're worth money to someone else. Just be careful if you're flying solo, which I suspect you are."

Fortescue smiled. Pritchett had a copper's nose for trouble.

The next day, after arranging to hitch a ride early the following morning with an American unit going to Munich, he returned to the court building to have one last look through some remaining documents, even though he already knew he was unlikely to find what he was searching for. The black book Karin had given him, and which he had not yet scrutinised, was still in his bag beside him, wrapped in sheets of old newspaper.

As he left in the late afternoon, one of the guards on the main gate to the building handed him a note inside a dirty brown envelope. He opened it.

Meet me this evening at 6 o'clock at the river crossing at the western end of the Trödelmarktinsel. I have some information that may interest you.

There was no name at the bottom. Fortescue was briefly tempted to ask Pritchett to accompany him but he decided that would only oblige him to divulge more. He would go alone, armed as always with the army pistol he was entitled to carry until he reached Berlin.

It was not hard to spot the man who had asked to meet him.

"Major Fortescue, my name is Kellerman. I'm a detective with the police in Munich."

"If you're from Munich, why are you here?"

"I'm helping out – on temporary attachment."

He looked shifty, unconvinced by his own explanation, and offered no identification.

"I work closely with the Americans. We've been keeping an eye on you – looking out for your safety, you might say. Your friend, Major Steiner – one of the interrogators of those bastards – told us you were here."

"I must thank Major Steiner for his kindness when I next see him. But I'm small fry. Why aren't you focusing on some of those who have so far escaped the net of justice?"

Kellerman sidestepped the question.

"We have observed others – more hostile – interested in your movements and those of a young woman with whom you spent some time in Munich but who it appears is now under US lock and key in Berlin. There was a double murder in the flat she occupied with a prostitute – Frieda, I think her name was – and the young woman's brother. If the Americans want the girl, so be it. We're interested in something that was in the flat and that seems to have disappeared – some documents, I understand – and who wants them. They could be ex-Nazis.

The local police at Seeshaupt discovered a body in the woods. We believe he was one of those instructed to follow you, though for what purpose is not clear. I don't expect you to know anything about that."

Kellerman's demeanour had changed – less solicitous. And he seemed well informed.

"I'm afraid I can't shed much light," Fortescue replied.

"Is that so?" countered Kellerman. He turned and pointed in the approaching dusk to a damaged building across the way. "Over there is the ancient executioner's house – or what now remains of it after the bombing. The house and the tower next to it were for centuries the official residence of the *Nachrichter* or city executioner. After the judge passed sentence, he carried out the punishment – whether it be public humiliation, corporal punishment or execution. What my colleagues and I wish to do is to pick up where you Allies left off – to hunt down those who have so far escaped justice for their crimes, to become their executioner. If you have information, you can help us."

They walked towards the ruin.

"How do I know, Herr Kellerman, that you are who you say you are?"

The detective pulled from his pocket a dog-eared police identity card.

"I'm afraid there is little I can add to what you seem to know already. Yes, I did meet the young woman in question and we did spend a couple of days together. But then she went to Berlin with the Americans. I don't know her whereabouts."

Fortescue deliberately did not mention Karin's name. As Kellerman had not mentioned it, it was possible he did not know it.

"I think you know more than you're telling me. May I ask when you are leaving the city?"

"Early tomorrow morning," replied Fortescue.

Kellerman paused. "I have one task you may be able to help me with."

"And what is that?" asked Fortescue.

"Light a cigarette and as you do so turn slowly and look towards the bridge. You will see a man in a long coat, turned-up collar and wearing a hat. He followed you here. I would like to speak to him but to do so I need to get to a place where I can corner him out of public view. Do you know the church in Sebalder Platz?"

Fortescue turned. He could not be sure but the man – the angle at which he wore his hat – was vaguely similar to the man who had watched his billet in Munich, the man Karin had seen and the sight of whom had prompted her to stay. He turned back to Kellerman.

"Yes. I've been there several times to admire the nave – the nave with no roof."

"Good. I suggest that you go there in half an hour's time. Sit near the front of the nave, close to one of the large candles. He will undoubtedly follow you in. When he does, my sergeant and I will grab him. Then you can go."

"Why don't you and your sergeant arrest him now?"

"In matters of this sort we have to be discreet."

"Why?" countered Fortescue.

"In these difficult times, that's the way it is. In half an hour, Major Fortescue, inside the church, that's where we'll meet."

Fortescue nodded. As Kellerman walked away, Fortescue looked again at the ruined executioner's house, imagining some of the tortured souls who had perished in front of its door. And then there was the charnel house – not far as the crow flew – where as a reluctant, uneasy voyeur he had recently seen the bodies of those he had helped to convict laid out for gruesome inspection after execution, some with the rope still around their necks.

Chilled by his recollection, Fortescue turned towards Sebalder Platz, stopping for a drink on the way. A pretty young woman approached him.

"My name is Elke. Are you free tonight? Do you want some companionship? I don't charge much."

"I have to meet someone soon but I'm happy to buy you a drink."

"Meeting another girl?" she asked.

"No. A man. We've got some business to discuss."

He and the girl sat talking at the bar for twenty minutes or more. He felt sorry for her. She didn't have a job; her father had been killed on the Eastern Front; and her mother took in laundry to wash.

"Look, Elke, you're a nice girl. Here's some money – not much, but save it for a rainy day or put it with other money and try to escape. I wish I could do more."

She blushed.

"Thank you, whoever you are. No one has done anything like this for me before." She kissed his cheek.

"I have to go now. I'm late."

"Which way are you going?"

"I'm going to the church in Sebalder Platz."

"May I walk with you? I live nearby."

He guessed she must have been only eighteen or nineteen. He hesitated but she took his arm. It made it difficult for him to turn to see if they were being followed.

"These streets are treacherous for a girl in heels," she said.

They walked quickly. She reminded him of Karin – the artless way she had taken his arm.

They reached the church.

"Goodbye, Elke. I wish you well."

"Thank you. You've been most kind. Goodbye." She kissed his cheek again and watched him enter the church. As he did so, he saw her hurry away.

The nave was bitterly cold and dark, apart from a few flickering candles. There was a large gaping hole in the roof through which Fortescue could see some stars. The pews were damp from an earlier shower. In front of him, near the apse, he saw three shadowy figures – three elderly women kneeling in prayer. He sat down several pews behind them. There was no sound except the drip of water from the empty space above. Images of falling bombs, the agonies of the injured, the terror of the fall of the accursed Third Reich, of burning, rape and murder passed across his mind. He looked up at the stars above. It had all come to this – devastation.

He heard approaching footsteps behind him. He turned. Though it was difficult to see in the darkness, he thought he saw the figure of Kellerman enter alone and sit three rows behind him. An aged priest approached the altar and began to say prayers for the city and the victims of war. The Mass – if it could be called that – lasted half an hour. Afterwards, the priest began to snuff out the candles. Fortescue approached him.

"Can you show me the tomb of St Sebaldus, founder of this church? I believe it was never removed for safe keeping during the war."

"Of course, young man, come with me. It's in the East Choir."

The priest spent several minutes explaining the history of the church.

"I have to leave now. Wherever you go, I wish you a safe journey."

"Thank you, Father. You have been most kind."

Fortescue walked in darkness down the side of the nave. He suddenly heard a scuffle and then a stifled cry. He lit his lighter but could see nothing untoward. He took a few further paces, holding the lighter up in front of him. The body was hanging from the iron bars of a side chapel. It was Kellerman, his throat cut, blood running down his leather coat and dripping onto the stone floor. Fortescue was suddenly pinned against a column, his arm twisted upwards behind his back.

"You will be next, Mr Prosecutor, if you don't lead us soon to the woman and what she and the others were given for safe keeping. Do you understand? We will follow you for as long as necessary to get what we want."

Fortescue was flung to the floor and kicked hard.

"Don't forget what I said."

His assaulter quickly disappeared into the night. Fortescue stumbled to his feet, his ribs numb with pain. He felt for his pistol. It was still there. Emerging from the church, he saw Elke.

"What are you doing here?" he snapped.

"I came back to the church to say a prayer for your generosity. Please don't be cross with me."

"I'm not Elke – just tired."

"Would you like to come to my home – it's just nearby – to eat something? After that you can go."

"Elke, I will walk you home but that's all. I must go back and pack my stuff. I have an early start in the morning."

Again, she held his arm – more tightly this time.

"Did you see anything unusual in the church?" he asked casually.

"A man came in and sat several pews ahead of me. Then another man entered, his collar turned up, and sat just in front of me. Because it was so dark, that's all I saw," she replied.

"Did you see their faces?"

"No," she said. "I told you it was too dark. Why are you asking me these questions? Are they after you? Are you in trouble?" she asked, looking at him earnestly.

"No," he answered, trying not to show his physical discomfort. "The best thing that's happened to me is meeting you – a pretty girl who would turn any man's head. If I were younger, I would ask you to be my girl."

She stopped and kissed him.

"Thank you so much. I live down this alley. Are you sure you won't come in?"

"No, Elke, go indoors and be safe."

She kissed him again and left. He watched her disappear down the cobbled street.

Early the next morning Fortescue had breakfast with Pritchett. They made arrangements to meet in London in the new year along with some other members of the prosecution team.

"But let's have a beer somewhere before then," said Pritchett.

"I would like that, Bob. In the meantime, thank you for all that you have done to look after me over the past year."

"It's been a pleasure. By the way, you're getting out at the right time. This morning the local police told me there were two murders last night – a man with dubious papers had his throat cut in the church in Sebalder Platz and a young girl received similar treatment near her home. They found over fifty US dollars in her handbag. It appears she was a prostitute. Are you all right, Richard? You look as white as a sheet."

"It's nothing, really. It's just that it's an awful way for a young girl to die – prostitute or not. I thought that after the trial this country would face a better future."

"It doesn't," replied Pritchett. "Now that the Americans have other fish to fry, it's up to the local police to handle these matters. They're not up to it yet."

"It seems so," murmured Fortescue.

Two hours later he was on his way back to Munich. Ahead of him went a telegram to British headquarters in Berlin, from Pritchett, reporting his suspicions and recommending that Major Richard Fortescue be interviewed on arrival about possible information he might be withholding.

CHAPTER FIVE

Recall to Berlin

Fortescue waited two days for a seat on a US military aircraft to Berlin. Dorothy had offered to intervene to get him on an earlier flight but he insisted on taking his place in the queue. Although he was eager to complete the journey and re-establish contact with Karin, he did not want to make a fuss or draw attention to himself.

While waiting his summons to the airfield, he sat down with his black notebook to chronicle his movements since his first encounter with her in the bar – in more detail this time, and with more calculated a purpose. He knew from his army training and from his interrogation experience in Nuremburg, observing the way some of the defendants had prepared, that it was essential to memorise the story you wished to present to the inquisitor. Adopting the same approach, he wished to ensure there would be no gaps in his alibi, no inconsistencies, that others might seek to exploit for their own motives. To reinforce his story, he decided that his diary should be selective in its record so that if it were taken from him its contents would not lead to his undoing. It therefore did not record the shot he had fired at Seeshaupt, apparently killing the man who had pulled a gun on him and Karin. Nor did his diary record his encounter with Elke, the young prostitute. However, it recounted his meeting with the man who called himself

Kellerman and what had happened to him. There was one other problem. He had a bullet missing from his gun. Under regulations he should report use of his firearm, the circumstances in which the shot was fired. He would have to find a convincing excuse if challenged or find a replacement bullet.

Before leaving Munich, he took Dorothy Maddox to lunch – not that you could call it lunch. It was thin soup, some bread and a piece of stale cheese, washed down with some rough, almost undrinkable red wine. He had come to enjoy her company on the few occasions they had spent together in the short time he had been in Munich.

Tall and slim, she was in her late thirties, he guessed. She told him she had spent most of the war in London. Her husband, an RAF fighter pilot, had been shot down over Kent in late 1940, dying soon after from his injuries. With no children, she had decided to join the war effort and worked, she claimed, at the War Office. With a degree in modern languages from Oxford, she spoke impeccable French and was fluent in German, as he already knew. She let slip that she had briefly been involved in eavesdropping on the conversations of captured German officers in England but he suspected this was far from the full story. She had a proud but refined face, pensive eyes and fine hands. Her movements and mannerisms displayed a pleasing grace and fluidity and when she smiled her eyes sparkled, making her look young and striking. But after each smile, her face once again became a mask of inscrutability concealing impenetrable secrets, borne out by her aversion to questions, in response to which she would turn the subject and talk only of the more banal aspects of her life. Occasionally though, as on the night Karin had first stayed in his billet, she had fleetingly revealed a passionate, almost crusading belief in the cause of freedom, her hatred of oppression and her support for equality of opportunity, a world in which a woman would be respected as a woman. No sooner had she uttered these words than she slammed the book shut.

She was now, she said, on temporary attachment to the US military in Munich as an interpreter, but often doing various administrative chores. Smart in her uniform and with a dry sense of humour, she was, in Fortescue's judgement, a shrewd observer of human behaviour and excellent in repartee. She had proved a discreet colleague and, judging by the quality and style of the clothes she had persuaded Karin to buy, with excellent local contacts, even in the garment business.

"I'm sorry to see you go, Richard. It's been a pleasure to have a young, good-looking Brit around the place, even for such a short time. I hope we can keep in touch when you're back in London."

"I would like that," he replied. "You've been a trusted and tactful friend. I have told you things I have not told others."

"What you told me will go no further."

"Thank you. I've done things I should not have done."

"I know," she replied. "How is Fräulein Eilers?"

"As you're aware, she's now in Berlin with the Americans."

"I'm glad you helped her. She seemed to have had a rough time in the latter part of the war. Though she put a brave face on things, there was vulnerability behind it."

"I noticed that too," he said. "I've always had a weakness for vulnerable women," he added.

"Ah! So, you're the predator type!" said Dorothy with a smile.

"Far from it," he replied. "It takes one vulnerable person to spot another. Comfort in numbers."

The conversation paused. Fortescue knew what her next question would be.

"Are you going to see her in Berlin?"

"I don't know," he answered.

"Would you like to?"

He was tempted to reply that it was none of her business. But he thought better of it. He had few friends he could trust. He believed she was one he could, if the need arose.

"Yes. I would like to, if only to say a proper farewell. But I'm not sure that will be possible. I don't want to make life difficult for her by having a uniformed Brit around."

"Or for yourself," interjected Dorothy. "Besides, don't you have a pretty girl waiting for you in London?"

Fortescue blushed slightly.

"Yes. Susannah. I've heard that she may come to Berlin shortly. Her father seems to have got her a seat on an RAF transport. So you see, I don't want to muddy the waters. You know what I mean."

"Yes," replied Dorothy with a hint of wistfulness, "I know what you mean. It happens – the unexpected – to all of us. And the little book she had? What of that?" she asked in an almost casual manner, as though it was an afterthought. Nothing was an afterthought with Dorothy, he mused. Every remark of any substance was planned. What was he to say?

"She took it with her."

Whether Dorothy believed him he could not say.

After some further conversational pleasantries, they finished their unspeakable wine and walked towards the English Garden – far from the beautiful place it had once been – talking about this and that.

"Richard, I don't know all that happened between you and Fräulein Eilers – and there is no need for you to tell me. We all have secrets, and those between a man and a woman can be disclosed only by them. What I do know is that the police have been keen to talk to someone fitting her description about the two bodies in the flat where you said she lived. You appear in her life – by accident, as I know. She's an attractive young woman who would turn any man's head, as she may have done yours. And why should she not? I'm not questioning your judgement. Each of us should be free to live our life as we would wish, away from prying eyes. But if the police enquiries follow you to Berlin and you need my help, just contact me. I'll be here for the next few weeks before possibly going to Berlin myself and then perhaps eventually back to London." She squeezed his arm – a kind of maternal gesture a mother might give a departing child. "Don't forget, Richard, call me – however slight the need. I keep secrets. That's my business – even dirty ones."

He took her hands in his and kissed her cheek. He sensed she already knew what had happened at Seeshaupt and possibly at Nuremburg. How, he did not know.

"Thank you, Dorothy. I won't forget you. I'm not sure how my complicated life will work out but it is reassuring to know I have a friend I can trust."

"A true friend, Richard, a true friend, would be a better description. As we're finding out, allies can be unreliable and duplicitous."

They embraced each other and as they did so he felt her put something in his pocket. They parted, going their different ways. Before reaching his billet, he took the small brown envelope out of his pocket. He opened it. Inside was a tightly folded piece of paper wrapped around something hard. He unwrapped it. It was a bullet, similar to the one he had fired in Seeshaupt. He read the few words on the paper.

> *You may need this.*
> *Be steady.*
> *Call me if you need help.*
> *Dorothy*

He carefully refolded the paper with the bullet inside. How on earth did she know?

That night he updated his diary and ensured that Karin's book was safely secreted in the lining of his battered leather holdall to which was tied a heavily printed label: *British Delegation to the Nuremburg War Tribunal.* Also in the bag, beneath some clothing, was the ashtray the market vendor had given him and the stained copy of *Mein Kampf* with the swastika armband inside. This was one bag he would not allow the nosy RMPs in Berlin to open.

It was a long and noisy flight to Berlin, with an intermediate stop in Frankfurt. On arrival late that evening, Fortescue was met by a jeep and driven to his billet at high speed through gloomy streets that intersected a wasteland of devastated buildings with the appearance of empty matchboxes. His accommodation was not far from British military headquarters at Lancaster House and its neighbouring buildings, Cumberland House and York House. The night orderly handed him some messages – mainly listing some calls he was required to make the next day, full details of which he would receive in the morning from Colonel Paycock, Chief of Staff to the British Commandant. Fortescue noticed that amongst the housekeeping names were two he had heard of. The first was Colonel Spires, responsible for garrison personnel security, and the other was Charles Nolan. The first he could handle with ease but the second caused him a slight shiver of apprehension. Nolan bore intelligence responsibility. The orderly added, almost as a casual aside, that Major Max Steiner, US army, was anxious to speak to him about an urgent matter.

"Where can I make a private phone call, Corporal?"

"In the cubicle over there, Sir," he replied.

Fortescue closed the door and picked up the phone.

A female operator answered.

"I wish to speak to Major Steiner, US army, on the following phone number."

"I'll call you back, Sir."

"Be as quick as you can."

"I will. The switchboard is busy tonight."

Fortescue paced the corridor. Five minutes later the phone rang. Making sure the cubicle door was firmly closed behind him and remembering to keep the call as short as possible, he picked up the receiver. He heard Steiner's familiar drawl.

"Hey, Rich, what took you so long to get here?"

"Flights were busy. I had to wait for a seat on a plane. How are you?"

"Under pressure," Steiner snapped back. "You and I need to meet in the morning. I've got to get that something – you know what – off my hands. It's beginning to cause me a problem because –"

Fortescue interrupted.

"I know, Max. I'm happy to help but don't give me the details now. Let's meet tomorrow morning. I'll be fresh by then. My first appointment is at 9.30 a.m. with the Chief of Staff but after that I'm free for a couple of hours before I have to see my Commandant, Major-General Nares."

There was a pause the other end.

"OK. Let's say 10.30 a.m. in the PX. It's noisy but we won't be overheard."

"I'll be there."

"Don't be late, Rich. I want to shift this cargo – quickly."

"I understand, Max. I understand. I'll be there."

"You'd better."

Fortescue put the phone down and climbed the stairs to his room. He'd just entered and was turning the key when there was a knock on the door. It was the orderly.

"There was one more message for you, Sir. It got mixed up with some others."

"Thank you, Corporal. Could you do me a favour? I've had a long flight. I'd love a double whisky to send me to sleep. Can you bring one up?"

"Certainly, Major. I'll put it on your tab."

With the whisky beside him, he opened the telegram.

> *Darling Richard*
> *Due in Berlin the day after tomorrow*
> *Can't wait to kiss you*
> *Much to talk about and plan*
> *All my love*
> *Susie*

He crumpled the message. What a bloody mess he was in.

After a restless sleep, he got up early and, following a brisk walk to clear his head, reported to Colonel Paycock at 9.30 a.m.

"Good to see you at last. We were beginning to wonder where you had got to. Sir Hartley Shawcross passed through here recently and spoke highly of you. Seems he's keen to see you at work in a Whitehall legal department. I'm sure there would be an equally good slot for you in the army. But you can decide that later. As I think you know, General Thomas's daughter has managed to get a place on an RAF plane tomorrow. The RAF at Gatow will have her details. Apparently, you and she are going to get engaged. That should help your army career if you decide to stay."

Fortescue made no comment.

"The Commandant looks forward to meeting you at 12.15. He's keen to hear your account of the executions at Nuremburg – whether the Yanks did indeed shorten the drop, to give the buggers a slow, painful death."

Steiner was waiting impatiently for Fortescue.

"You're late, Rich. What kept you out of Berlin?"

"This and that and checking-in procedures, as you well know," replied Fortescue in a casual manner.

"Look, I need to get your girlfriend off my hands quickly. She's your property, not mine. I've managed to keep her presence a secret from my security people but not for much longer. Having a German broad around is not welcome, could stir up trouble. She is staying in a house found by a friend of a friend. I don't think she's happy there and she's threatened to leave more than once. Another problem is that some guys seem to be watching the place. It's not clear who they are. Could be the so-called German cops, or black-market types, or possibly Russians seeking fresh blood for their brothels in the East. And not least, she's costing me room money. So, Rich, when are you going to take her away?"

"I'll do my best to come for her tomorrow night. But she may have to stay there a day or so longer. I need time to find somewhere secure for her to stay in our sector."

"You must make it tomorrow. I don't want any embarrassment from any connection between her and me, given my role in pursuing Krauts. And as I've warned you, she might just leave. Something seems to be bugging her. Perhaps she's pining for you. One way or another she's on your tab after tonight. I've more than repaid my favour to you."

"I know, Max. Tomorrow night it will be – without fail."

"Great. I'll join you for a drink at the Officers' Club at 8.30 p.m. and we'll go on from there."

Fortescue's conversation with Major-General Nares went as he had predicted. The Commandant's eagerness to hear about the conduct of the Nuremburg executions meant the twenty minutes allotted for the meeting sped past without any awkward questions. The next appointment was different.

Charles Nolan was a tall gaunt-faced man with thin grey hair and equally thin lips. Formerly a superintendent at Scotland Yard and now part of the British intelligence operation in Berlin, since his arrival in the city he had quickly gained a reputation for forensic questioning as part of the increasing effort to ensure that all sensitive information was well protected by those given access to it – and did not fall into Soviet hands.

After standing to greet his visitor, Nolan sat down behind a large uncluttered desk, a single file in front of him. To Fortescue, his unsmiling face and gimlet eyes behind steel-framed glasses added to the impression of a humourless inquisitor. He was the archetypal image of a Reich senior official. His appearance, and the starkness of the wood-panelled room, would have easily fitted the descriptions of Gestapo interrogation sessions recounted by witnesses to the tribunal. Clearly seeking to put Fortescue at ease, Nolan asked him in short clipped sentences for his impressions of the tribunal – what he had learned of the German psyche that could have provoked such evil and how each of the principal defendants had reacted to their conviction and sentence. He was also interested in the Soviet delegation at Nuremburg – whom he had met, what their specific role had been, how they relaxed. They talked about London and Fortescue's future plans. Fortescue heard the clock ticking noisily and remorselessly on the mantelpiece behind him, eating into the time he needed to find a place for Karin. As the pale sunlight began to shine through the window behind the desk, he began to see only the outline of his inquisitor's face, making it increasingly difficult for him to judge the impact of his answers. The conversation paused as Nolan turned over two sheets of paper in the file. Fortescue sensed he was about to strike.

"You're highly regarded in London. It's evident many would like to avail themselves of your talent."

"I can only take your word for it," replied Fortescue.

There was another pause. Then he struck.

"Tell me about Fräulein Karin Eilers. I think you met her in Munich recently. Is she a casual acquaintance or something more?"

Fortescue, trying to hide his surprise that Nolan should know, replied with care.

"I was having a coffee in a bar one morning, near the National Theatre. She walked in, sat down and was about to light a cigarette. The bartender hassled her – she had to buy something to drink or leave. She became distressed. I bought her a coffee. We got talking and that evening she joined me at the opera, for which I had a spare ticket. I accompanied her home, saying goodbye to her in the downstairs hallway. As I was leaving, I heard a scuffle above. I ran upstairs to find a man assaulting her. I hit him and took her back to my accommodation for her safety. I reported her presence to Dorothy Maddox. Miss Eilers and I spent the next few days together, talking about this and that, doing nothing in particular. Then she left the city."

Nolan paused, writing on a pad he'd produced from the desk drawer and placed squarely beside the file.

"What was the address – of the place she called home?"

"I don't recall, as it was she who directed the taxi driver and there was almost no street lighting. There are few street signs in Munich. Just like here. But it was not far from the main station."

"After she was attacked, did she or you go into the flat?"

"No," replied Fortescue.

Nolan wrote again on the notepad.

"Did you know that the local police were looking for someone fitting her description – that they wished to talk to her to see if she might be able to help them in connection with two bodies in the flat where she had apparently lived until you took her under your wing?"

"I read about it in the local newspaper, which she drew to my attention."

Nolan paused to write yet again. Fortescue tried to mask his discomfort. He had twice misled Nolan. He had gone into the flat; he had seen the bodies and he knew their identity. The ticking clock was beginning to irritate him.

Nolan looked up.

"Did you sleep with the Fräulein?"

"Yes," replied Fortescue. "Twice."

"Did she tell you anything during your moments of intimacy?"

"No," Fortescue snapped.

"Why did you suddenly go back to Nuremburg when you had already concluded your work there and taken leave of your colleagues?"

"I had read something in the Munich newspapers. It triggered a recollection of some tribunal evidence and I wanted to go back and check one or two documents I had seen during the preparation for the trial. But I was too late. What may have helped me had gone – on their way to Washington."

"What had triggered your recollection?"

"It was a reference to a code. I wanted to be clever and solve it. But I couldn't."

"I see. Where is Fräulein Eilers now?"

"I understand she is in Berlin," replied Fortescue.

"And her whereabouts in Berlin?" came the instant next question.

"I think the Americans are looking after her."

"You think, or you know for certain?"

Fortescue paused.

"I'm pretty certain."

Nolan wrote again, in silence.

"Since you are acquainted with Fräulein Eilers – perhaps more intimately than you have so far explained but we won't go into that now – we would like you to bring her under our protection as soon as possible. We will explain why later."

"If that is what you wish, I will do my best."

"It is certainly what we wish. She may hold the key to an unsolved problem, the nature of which I am not at liberty to disclose."

Fortescue made no comment.

"We'll arrange some suitable discreet accommodation. But as

she probably only trusts you, it is better that you prise her from the Americans, assuming they have her, or, if they don't, that they know where she can be found. You will receive further instructions shortly."

Fortescue was about to get up when Nolan said he had one last question.

"Have you had cause to use your sidearm?"

"Why do you ask?"

"Routine. That's all. May I see it, please?"

Fortescue drew the weapon from its holster and handed it to Nolan, who smelt the barrel and checked the chamber.

He made a note and then returned the gun.

"Ah! There is one other thing."

"And what is that?" asked Fortescue, trying hard to suppress his now intense irritation.

"I believe your fiancée, Miss Thomas, will arrive in Berlin imminently. How do you intend to manage a *ménage à trois*, if you are able to persuade Fräulein Eilers to accompany you?"

"First, Miss Thomas is not my fiancée as I have yet to propose to her. Second, how I intend to manage a *ménage à trois* – to use your term of art – is for me to decide. May I go now?"

"Yes, you may go, but before you do so, let me summarise your position. First, you didn't return to Berlin at the appointed time, but that's a matter between you and your superiors. Second, it seems you have slept with a German woman whose mother was in the circle around Goebbels. Third, I have reason to believe you are withholding certain information about people you may have encountered not just in Munich but in Nuremburg as well. However, for the present, the matter rests here in this file. I will not pass it to your army superiors or to mine. Our principal preoccupation is to seek your help in persuading Fräulein Eilers to join you in our sector and then, with your encouragement, she might be able to shed some light on what happened to her mother. Do you understand what you have to do?"

"Yes," replied Fortescue.

He left the room, his hands damp with sweat. He had lied and had indeed withheld important information. But he had also discovered a fact that Karin had not disclosed to him at

58

Seeshaupt: that her mother may have been more significant in the Nazi hierarchy – provided, of course, Nolan's information was correct. What puzzled him, though, was why his superiors had not simply asked the Americans for permission to talk to Karin. Why should her transfer from the US to the British sector be a task for him? And Nolan was clearly well informed. Where did his information come from? And, surprisingly, if he knew so much, why had he not mentioned the existence of the black book and asked who had it now? Putting these questions aside, he turned to other pressing matters.

The next evening, in a dilapidated house in the US sector, Fortescue waited in a shabby sitting room. He heard movement above. A few minutes later Karin entered the room, wearing the dress that Dorothy had bought for her in Munich. Her face was expressionless, no flicker of emotion. He motioned her to sit down and offered a cigarette. She accepted one. He lit it.

"How are you?" he asked.

"As well as can be expected," she replied in a soft, almost inaudible voice. "I spend most of each day in my room – confined to barracks, I think you say in the military – reading dreadful American magazines. Yesterday – or perhaps it was the day before – I went for a short walk. But I thought I was being followed so I returned."

"You were wise to do so."

"I've decided that it would be best for me to go back to Munich as soon as possible – to a city I know, unlike this dump. There's nothing for me here."

"I think you should stay in Berlin."

"Why should I do that?"

"Because you'll be safer here and besides, I'm here."

"I thought you were going back to London."

"Not for the present. There's been a change of plan."

She gave a hollow laugh.

"Stuck in a ruined city that I cannot leave – is that what you call freedom?"

"Karin, I would like to help you. I can make arrangements for your future. They will be better."

"That's what you said in Seeshaupt – you would help me. The result is this place."

"Karin, you have to stay."

"Why do I have to stay? So that you can fuck me to your heart's content each night? Is that what you want? And me – waiting for crumbs of physical comfort from your table?"

"Why are you so bloody cynical? My motives are honourable. How can you still doubt that? Yes, I like you. Indeed, I more than like you. But what I remember was the fear you showed the night you were attacked. Berlin is no place for you, nor is Munich. London might be."

"And be a hated alien in the country of the victors? History is written by the victors. Are you writing a script for me – a script where I will always be at the mercy of the victorious?"

"Karin, please stop being so damn negative!" He paused. "The war is over and, though I barely know you, you have turned my world upside down. I don't know how. But that is the truth of the matter. You may not care for me – ever. But that does not stop me – out of pure altruism – out of love – wishing to help you. So, I ask you – I implore you – please stay and let me help."

She looked at him, her face frozen, unable to speak. He took her hands and pulled her to her feet, embracing her tightly in his arms.

"Please let me help you."

She buried her face in his shoulder.

"If only you could, Richard, if only you could," she whispered.

"I can and I will. I won't let you down. Early tomorrow I will come and take you to a safe and comfortable place in the British sector. Get some sleep in the meantime and have your things ready to leave by eight o'clock in the morning."

She nodded. They kissed, her face still moist with tears. A short while later he left to check the address that Nolan's office had sent him late in the afternoon.

Early the next morning he was awoken by the orderly with an urgent message to call Steiner.

"Rich, why the hell didn't you take her with you last night, as you said you would?"

"Her safe accommodation was not yet ready. Why, what's the matter?"

"Rich, you're too bloody late. She was taken in the early hours."

"Who took her, Max? Who?"

"I don't know. The concierge just heard some muffled shouts and by the time she had got out of bed and downstairs she saw her being bundled into a car."

"And the number plate?" asked Fortescue.

"It was too dark to see. The police are at the house now. If you want more information, call them. I've done my bit. If you want her, she's your problem, Rich, not mine."

The line went dead.

He asked to see Nolan without delay.

"Major, that's unfortunate. But we still want her assistance. And I am sure she will still be in the city. We'll trace her whereabouts – our own sources may well have intelligence on this development. Once we've done so, we will need you to get her and bring her to our sector. You seem to be the only one she trusts. Meanwhile, you had better prepare for Miss Thomas's arrival tomorrow."

Fortescue cursed silently.

During the course of the day, he turned what had happened over and over in his mind. He was torn. He believed he was falling in love with her. He wanted her to be with him. But if she had gone for good, then so be it. He would have to accept it. Let her be a footnote in his life; turn a new page. Let others pursue her if they so wished. Why should she complicate his life any further? But however hard he tried, he could not get her out of his mind. She was becoming his obsession.

CHAPTER SIX

Return to the Past

As he drove to the RAF base at Gatow, on the city's outskirts, to meet Susannah Thomas, Fortescue reflected on times past and times to come.

Born in 1914 – the youngest of two brothers and a sister – into a prosperous Norfolk family, he had spent his early years in rural comfort despite the ravages of the First World War, which had cost his father's life at the Battle of Passchendaele in the autumn of 1917. At the age of thirteen, in 1927, arranged by his uncle, Charles Fortescue, he had started to board at Stowe School in Buckinghamshire. Established in 1923 at the former country seat of the Dukes of Buckinghamshire and Chandos, it sought to present itself as a modern public school focused on the grounding of the individual without the disagreeableness of fagging and other archaic practices prevalent at more historic public schools. After initial homesickness, Fortescue had enjoyed life at Stowe and soon displayed an aptitude for modern languages. Before long he became head boy of his school house. In 1932, his ageing uncle again intervened and he went up to Peterhouse in Cambridge, graduating with honours in 1935. Following a year of doing nothing, he joined a London publishing house, translating German texts, especially poetry. In 1938, bored in London, he went to Germany where, thanks to a small bequest from his uncle, he was able to stay for several months, visiting Berlin, Munich and Dresden, ostensibly for the purpose of identifying young German writers whose works might be suitable for translation in England. But it was soon apparent this would be hard in the virulent climate of the Third Reich.

After witnessing Hitler's triumphant return to Berlin at the beginning of October 1938, following the Munich Agreement with the Prime Minister, Neville Chamberlain, and with his resources dwindling, Fortescue returned to London in December. Disturbed by what he had seen and still undecided which career he should follow, he applied for a commission in the army, much to his mother's dismay. He joined the Royal Norfolk Regiment and went briefly with them to India. By 1940 the regiment had returned to England. It was not long afterwards that his fluency in German led to his secondment to the Inter-Service Department of MI6. From there he had been handpicked to join the British team for the Nuremburg war crimes tribunal as an interrogator and interpreter.

Now, at the age of thirty-two, he was at another crossroads, uncertain whether to stay in the military, to apply for the Foreign Office or perhaps accept an offer from his old school to become a language teacher. But more pressing was the question of whether he wished to marry his girlfriend, Susannah Thomas. She was expecting a proposal of marriage, which in her parents' view was long overdue.

A slim and attractive woman, a typical English rose, Susannah was five years younger than him; they had met at a party in London on his return from Germany. She came from a distinguished military family: her father and his father and grandfather had each reached senior rank in the army. The prospect of her marrying a highly regarded and talented young officer filled her parents with pleasure. Susannah had a restrained sense of humour and a slightly irritating laugh, but she was nonetheless amusing company and many regarded the two of them as a perfect couple. They had seen each other intermittently during the war – her father had found her an administrative job in the War Office; in between, they had corresponded regularly. On their last weekend together before he had gone to Nuremburg, she had professed her love for him and hoped that once the war was over they might marry and perhaps have children. Fortescue had been circumspect in his reply but she had interpreted his "Let's see" response, accompanying smile and their two nights together in a dismal hotel in Brighton as tantamount to an engagement at the war's end. On her arrival in Berlin, he knew he could no longer avoid a decision.

He watched the plane taxi to a stop. Her failure to disembark early led him to think she may have been denied a seat at the last moment. Then she appeared, suitably wrapped in a thick black coat and wearing a fur hat. Both the hat and her high heels made her seem taller than before as they embraced each other, she giving him several passionate kisses reminiscent of some of the amorous poses in the *Picture Post* magazine on VE Day. She placed her arm in his as they were driven into Berlin.

Fortuitously, that evening there was a dinner dance at the British Officers' Club, so enabling Fortescue to avoid Susannah's inevitable question. That night she stayed at the Commandant's house while he remained in his own billet. He woke in the early hours and, unable to get back to sleep, got up, Susannah on his mind but Karin too. Where had she gone? Had she disappeared of her own volition or had she been abducted? Would he ever see her again? He missed her – not so much with an ordinary sense of loss of someone's company but with that inner ache that surely signalled a deeper longing. What was he going to do?

* * * * *

Two days before, two men, unpleasant in appearance and demeanour, had come for Karin early in the morning. The moment she saw them she knew who they were and why they had come and that it would be foolish to resist. As they waited downstairs, she quickly washed, dressed and packed her small battered leather suitcase, ensuring that the dusky-red dress with the velvet collar and waistband was neatly folded. Since she would not see Richard Fortescue again, the dress would be a lasting reminder of their short friendship. Closing her case she remembered dancing with him in front of the fire at Seeshaupt to the music of Beethoven. She had never experienced such gentleness, such sophisticated physical proximity with no threat of violence. She had felt her cynicism dissolve, though her vigilance for a possible opponent remained. She recalled too a moment at the start of that evening when it had seemed as though her challenge as to his motives had momentarily made him defensive. Sitting opposite her, a tall, powerfully built, good-looking man with a fresh complexion, wide, pale-blue eyes and sandy-coloured hair, he had exuded natural charm and courtesy. But what he must have seen and heard at Nuremburg had obviously cast a permanent shadow over him. In the short time they had been acquainted, she had observed that, while ready to smile and laugh, his eyes – in more sombre moments – revealed an almost unfathomable depth of thought. He was light-hearted one moment, serious the next. She imagined many women must have been drawn to him. She detected that he used a show of reserve to keep people at arm's length and avoid commitment. He had already confided that he was at heart a nomad of no fixed address – just like her. That was one bond between them. And yet she had been so cruel to him the night before – the wounding words. She tried hard to suppress her tears.

The car in which she was driven threaded its way past large areas of wasteland beneath which were buried shattered windows, broken doors, the rafters of roofs. She could not bear the thought of what awaited her. They arrived eventually at a large run-down house in Grunewald – not far from the S-Bahn station from which thousands of Jews had been transported to the East even in the early weeks of 1945. The shabby house appeared relatively unscathed, though the garden was unkempt. The curtains in every window were drawn. They went inside. It was as cold inside as it was outside. There was little sound, but a strong smell of cooking.

"Follow me," said a thickset man with grizzled hair, emerging from the shadow of the long corridor. Instead of going upstairs, he led her downstairs into a large, dank cellar. In the dim light, there seemed to be several brick-walled rooms, like monastic cells, each with a wooden door. She noticed that the door of one of them, towards the back of the cellar, was open. She could hear a scratched recording of some pre-war Berlin music. She was pushed from behind into the room. It was stuffy with a strong smell of sweat. A frayed fragment of worn carpet lay on the stone floor. To the left was a small wooden table bearing a plate of unfinished food and the gramophone, now stopped; the corner beyond was hidden by a thin curtain. A miserable fire burned in the fireplace and above the mantelpiece a torn and stained swastika flag was nailed to the wall. To the right was a truckle bed with a heap of blankets on it. Beside the fire was a small threadbare armchair. Sitting in it was the person she had expected to see – her mother.

"Ah, Karin! At last I have the pleasure of my daughter's company. Helmut, find her a chair so she can sit with me. She and I have much to talk about. Then leave us."

Her mother had aged significantly since she had last seen her in Berlin in October 1943. Karin recalled how, on that particular evening, she had been in buoyant mood, stylishly dressed in a tight-fighting wraparound silk dress allegedly given her by Magda Goebbels as a present for loyalty to her husband. She had talked excitedly of her invitation to celebrate the Minister's forty-sixth birthday and of the prospect of Hitler, Himmler and other top Nazis being there. Picking up a small suitcase and leaving some money on the table, she had warned Karin that afterwards she had important work to do that might occupy her for several weeks. But she was welcome to stay in Berlin, or at the house near Potsdam, where she would be well looked after by her maid, Brigitte. As the weeks passed with no sign of her mother, and as Karin became disenchanted with life in Berlin, particularly once Allied bombing of the city intensified, she left a note with Brigitte to say that she had returned to Frieda's, in Munich. Some time later her mother had replied, unapologetic for her lack of communication but promising to see her soon in Munich on one of her visits to the Berghof. In the spring of 1944 she received a further letter, enclosing a photo of her sitting next to Hitler. Later that year an SS officer had come to see Frieda to inform her that in due course she would receive, with the approval of Helga Eilers, certain sensitive documents to be kept in the flat.

Sitting opposite her, her mother was a shadow of her former self. She wore crumpled grey slacks, tucked into scuffed black boots, and a stained dark-green jumper too big for her. Her long hair was now grey. On her right middle finger, she wore what appeared to be a diamond ring set in the shape of a swastika. Her eyes were sunken and her face heavily lined. But she still seemed to radiate that intense inner fire that had driven her for so many years. Karin said nothing.

"Thank you for coming."

"It seems I had no choice," replied Karin.

Her mother let the comment pass.

"I need your help. I know I neglected you badly but there was so much to do. I was under such great pressure to succeed at what they wanted from me. I could not slip up. Will you forgive me?"

Karin looked at her mother, struggling inwardly with her emotions. Should she forgive or damn her?

Helga reached to touch her daughter's hand. Karin withdrew it.

"I cannot forgive you. You turned your back on Gerhard and me. He's dead – brutally murdered, if you didn't know – and I was left alone. All because you chose to put the Party before your family. I don't know what you did for them but you didn't care about us. How can I possibly forgive you? You should go to hell – you and everyone else from that accursed regime that has left Germany in tatters."

"Gerhard was not my son," Helga replied. "He was your father's bastard son. I took pity on him and brought him up after your father was killed. As for choosing the Party, everyone misunderstood the Führer. He worked so hard and, in the end, he was betrayed. I was with him in the bunker and I promised him and the Minister that I would remain loyal to the end. And loyal I will be to their memory – even now."

"You are a stupid, misguided woman with no conscience. Despite all that has been revealed about the crimes the Nazis committed, you still revere their memory. How can you possibly be so blind, so naive?"

Her mother did not respond. Karin's words seemed to have little impact. Helga just gazed into the fire, her thoughts seemingly elsewhere. Then she spoke.

"I have to leave Berlin. I cannot stay here any longer. I must breathe fresh air. There are a few friends left who can get me away to a safe place, as they have done others. But if they are to do so, I first need to retrieve the papers that were left for safe keeping at the flat in Munich. Others want them and therefore they will have a monetary value for me – my ticket to freedom."

"The papers are long gone," said Karin. "Taken by those who murdered my friend, Frieda, and Gerhard, and who tried to kill me. If you know who the killers were, ask them."

Her mother looked at her. She cursed.

"I asked you – via a messenger – to keep a small black book. Did they take that too?"

"No," Karin answered. "It's here in Berlin, but not in my hands."

"Who has it?" her mother asked anxiously. "I want it urgently."

"A friend has it."

"Who is this friend?"

"I cannot say."

"Karin, I want you to get it back from your friend and to give it to me personally – and as soon as possible."

"I cannot do that."

"Why?" her mother implored.

"Because I'm here – under duress – and he's in the British military."

Helga's face turned white and then contorted in anger.

"How on earth could you call an enemy officer your friend, let alone allow him to take the book I entrusted to you?"

"Because he saw it in my bag after he had rescued me from being raped and possibly murdered."

"You have to get it back – quickly. My friends will help you. Lure your military friend to a secluded place and we'll do the rest."

"You're mad. Why don't you give yourself up? Face trial and serve your sentence."

"That will never happen," her mother said angrily.

"I hope they catch you."

"With your help, they won't. Now, write a message to this so-called friend and Helmut will deliver it and wait for the book. Once I have it you can go and I will leave here – disappear."

"No," replied Karin. "I will deliver the message myself. I will get the book and return it. Once that is done, I never wish to see you again."

"Likewise," said her mother.

The argument between them raged for some minutes. Then they fell silent.

The following morning, after a sleepless night in the damp cellar, Karin left the house in the company of Helmut. They drove towards the city centre, where they got stuck in traffic in the Kurfürstendamm. Suddenly, she opened the car door and leapt out, running as fast as she could to hide from her pursuer – one of the men who had escorted her to Grunewald and who had been following Helmut's car. Managing to give him the slip, she went into a shop.

"How can I help you?" asked the young assistant.

"I've just seen someone the authorities may be looking for. I need to make a phone call."

"Shall I call the police for you?"

"No. I need to speak personally to the British. I have a contact number."

Karin went into the cubicle at the back of the shop and dialled the number for Lancaster House.

"Who do you wish to speak to?" asked the operator.

"Major Fortescue, please," she said, trying to suppress her tears.

"I think he may have left the building. Let me check. Please hold the line."

"Is everything all right?" enquired the shop assistant.

"Yes," replied Karin.

Then she heard his voice. It was hard to remain composed.

"It's me. Karin."

"Karin! Where have you been? Are you all right?"

"Not really. I need your help – urgently. Can we meet somewhere?"

"Yes, of course. I'll come immediately. Tell me where you are. We'll go somewhere safe and we'll talk. I've got an appointment later today but I'll take care of you. I promise."

Half an hour later Karin was in a British car with Richard Fortescue, on the way to a hotel in Wilmersdorf, near Lancaster House, often used, he explained, by visiting families of British personnel.

"What did you do with the black book I gave you?"

"I still have it."

"I would like it back."

"Why?"

"Because someone wants it badly and if I don't give it to them they will kill me. Please give it to me. And then I will get out of your life."

"Of course, you can have it back. I don't want you to come to any harm. You're too precious for that."

They arrived at the hotel, where he booked her into a room.

"Now, rest! I will come to see you later this evening. Answer the door to no one. I will bring the book with me." He kissed her.

She lay on the bed, exhausted.

* * * * *

Fortescue received two messages on his return to British headquarters. The first was from Charles Nolan, wishing to see him urgently. The other was from Susannah, to say that she had arranged a table for two at the British Officers' Club at 7.30 p.m. and that the following evening they would be dining at the Commandant's residence.

"Have you any news of Miss Eilers?" Nolan asked.

How should he reply? Should he lie or tell the truth?

"Not yet," he replied.

"Your answer suggests you may be expecting news, or am I placing a meaning on your words you do not intend?"

"I have received information that she is alive and may contact me soon. Whether that information is plausible or not, I cannot say."

"And may I ask the source of your optimism?"

"You may not," said Fortescue sharply. "You told me earlier that you wished me to find her. You added that your own sources might have information. Obviously they have not because if they had you would undoubtedly have told me or even found her yourself. Neither has happened. I conclude it's still up to me."

Nolan bit his lip.

"Yes. Until I have information, it is indeed up to you. You know her and you have her trust. But time is not on your side. Her mother remains unaccounted for. As she was apparently close to Goebbels, and may even have been in the bunker during Hitler's last days, we want to find out whether Miss Eilers knows what happened to her. Her mother is a person of note. If she is still alive she may have important information to divulge under interrogation. From that we can see if she should stand trial. So, Fortescue, hurry up."

That evening, Fortescue and Susannah dined *à deux*. It was a pleasant occasion. The club was only half full and with the adjacent table free there was little chance of their being overheard. Over supper they caught up on time lost and wartime experiences and memories.

"The Commandant says there is little for you to do in Berlin and Daddy tells me the Attorney-General is keen to recruit you to his staff in London. So, Major Fortescue, when are you coming back to London and, even more important, when are we going to get married?"

"I have one last task to do on behalf of our intelligence people here. It's secret, which is why the Commandant does not know about it. That should be finished by Christmas and then I will return and we can begin our plans."

"I will hold you to that," replied Susannah. "If you're not back by the beginning of January I will ask my father to request the Commandant to place you under arrest for dereliction of duty and put you on the first available plane home. This must be the last time we are apart for Christmas."

"I agree to your terms, Miss Thomas."

She hugged him tightly before she got into the military car to return to the Commandant's house. "See you tomorrow evening," she said. "Indeed, see you tomorrow evening," he replied, and blew her a kiss.

He watched the car drive away and then returned to the club for a whisky before leaving to see Karin.

She was lying on the bed when he entered the room. She was wearing the red dress from Munich. Her eyes were puffy from crying. He kissed her on the cheek and lay on the bed beside her. She rested against him, her hand on his chest, clearly exhausted by whatever she had experienced. They did not speak. After lighting a cigarette, he reached for his overcoat and pulled from the inside pocket the black book with the *Waffen* SS symbol on the front. She leaned against the bedhead.

"Thank you, Richard."

"Who wants it?" he asked.

"I cannot say. Once they have it and I'm out of their grip, I will tell you."

He paused. How could he put this to her?

"I can't decipher – at least not yet – the code in the book. With time, I might still be able to break it. Then we will know its secret and I can decide if there is anything we need to do. If you give me more time with the book, I might find the answer. But you say that is not possible. You insist that you have to give it back immediately because if you don't you will be killed. Is that really the case?"

"Yes. I will be. I don't want to die. I just want to vanish."

"What if you give the book back and they still kill you because you know too much? Have you thought of that?"

She looked at him. Her face bore a haunted look.

"No," she replied. "But it doesn't matter. I am from the

kingdom of the damned and must pay the price of association with those who dwell there."

"What 'price of association'? What do you mean?" he asked.

"I cannot say," she said again.

"I will help you return the book so I can make sure you are safe."

"No, Richard, you must not do that. I must do this on my own."

"So be it," he replied, deciding to leave matters as they were – at least for now. He put the book down on the bedside table beside his watch and the other contents of his pocket.

They lay on the bed, facing one another, speaking not a word, her finger tracing his lips. She began to kiss him. He fondled her. Quickly aroused, she stripped, throwing her clothes with abandon on the floor, he likewise. They made love, she sensual and demanding, pinning him beneath her, uttering obscenities, refusing to release him, insisting he make her come again. It seemed as though she was driven by demons. Finally, she fell beside him, spent, locking herself in his arms. They fell asleep.

On waking, he turned to reach for her but she had gone. He put the light on to discover that his black notebook had gone too. In the dark and in her haste, he assumed, she had picked it up instead of the SS book he had returned to her. On the bedside table, she had left a scrap of paper on which she had written goodbye. He dressed quickly. Downstairs, he asked the woman on the desk what time his guest had left. At 4.30 a.m., came the answer. He asked if anyone had been waiting for her in the lobby. The reply startled him. The woman believed she had left with a Soviet official – at least, he had spoken German with a Russian accent and he looked like an official.

Fortescue declined breakfast at the hotel, relying on a coffee in the quiet of the morning room to clear his thoughts. Then there was a tap on his shoulder. He spun round. It was Dorothy Maddox.

"Dorothy! When did you arrive?"

"Late last night, early this morning – I can't remember. As I arrived a Russian vehicle drove off at high speed. I didn't know they frequented this part of town for their sexual needs. But don't let's talk about that. How are you?"

"I'm well. Susannah is here. She's staying with the Commandant. He's invited us to dinner tonight."

"I've been invited too. He thought I might like a break from the Americans in Munich. Besides, the Commandant and I got to know each other in London. I think Charles Nolan is going too. What a dislikeable man he is. Let's ride out together and have a gossip."

"I'd like that," he replied.

"What happened to Fräulein Eilers? Have you seen her in Berlin?"

"Yes," replied Fortescue. "I was with her last night. Here."

"Has she decided what to do?"

"Not yet. She said she was in trouble – under pressure. But she wouldn't say from whom."

"Did you sleep with her?"

Fortescue hesitated. He was about to place further trust in a woman he still did not know well.

"Yes," he replied. "I wanted to talk to her again this morning but she left while I was still asleep. I think she left with a Russian – at least, that is what the woman on the front desk said. Perhaps she left in the vehicle you saw. How the occupants knew she was here is a mystery – unless, of course, she told them."

"Or someone else did," interjected Dorothy. "There are few secrets in this city."

"What am I going to do about the girl on the desk? She's bound to gossip."

"Don't worry," said Dorothy. "I'll speak to her. She's on our payroll. Susannah will never know."

"Thank you, Dorothy."

"Do you want Miss Eilers back?" she asked.

"Yes," he whispered. "Besides, Nolan wants to talk to her about some missing high-ups in the regime she might know."

"Does he now," she commented.

"What should I do? Nolan is on my back."

"You go off and do what you have to do. I will get changed

and freshen up and then I will speak to the RMPs to see if we have any information about the Russian vehicle and its occupants when it left the western sector. We'll talk this evening on the way to the Commandant's. Before then you should tell Nolan."

* * * * *

That morning the house in Grunewald received a message that Fräulein Eilers, who had been followed by Helmut's people after she was spotted getting into a British military vehicle near the Kurfürstendamm the day before, had been seen leaving a hotel in Wilmersdorf just a few hours earlier, in a Russian vehicle, heading for East Berlin. Helga Eilers reacted with fury.

"Once again I've been betrayed – this time by my own daughter. Now I know how the Führer must have felt when he was betrayed by those damned generals. I gave a simple instruction. Take her to her British friend and, once he had given her the book, bring it back here. Instead, she spends the night in a hotel and under your noses goes with some Russians to East Berlin."

"She may have been abducted," Helmut replied.

This barely mollified her rage.

"Whether she was abducted or went of her own accord," shouted Helga, "I despise her. All she had to do was to retrieve the book and give it to me. Had she done that, she could have gone to hell for all I care."

"Frau Eilers, I urge you to get ready to leave here quickly. Your name is assuredly on the list of those who are believed to have been in the bunker at the time of the Führer's death and whose fate is as yet unaccounted for. If your daughter tells the Soviets where you are, they may ask the British to seize you – or come themselves."

Helga paced up and down the cellar, uttering profanities.

"Helmut, alert the chain of command that I may come soon, though I will hold out until the last possible moment. I must have the book. Its value is the key to my survival – to carrying on the struggle."

He paid no attention. She saw from his expression that he thought her a rambling, deluded woman.

CHAPTER SEVEN

The Wind from the East

Two meetings took place the next morning in Berlin – one in the East and one in British military headquarters.

Karin Eilers took the cigarette offered to her – an expensive American one. Major Kovalev, who had introduced himself as an agent in the Soviet Ministry of State Security, leaned across the table and lit it, his eyes fixed on hers.

"I'm glad you decided to co-operate with us – to respond positively to the proposal we passed to you yesterday. It will make things much easier – for you and for us."

"How did you know I was in Berlin?" she asked.

"Fräulein Eilers, that's not the way we play. We ask the questions, you provide the answers. However, since you wish to know, we received reliable information about your arrival in the city from one of our agents in West Berlin, whose name I cannot of course reveal. But – to put your mind at rest – it was not the British soldier with whom you slept last night."

Karin did not respond. She hoped her face remained impassive, masking the fear she felt. She exhaled a cloud of smoke between them but Kovalev continued to look at her intently with his cold, opaque, depthless eyes, judging, she supposed, how best he might breach her defences. He chose the classic male approach.

"You are a highly attractive woman, Fräulein Eilers. If you chose to work for us, to be one of our agents, you could have a comfortable flat in Moscow, enjoying all the things a young woman like you misses in this miserable city. I'm sure we can agree on mutually acceptable terms and speed you on your way."

"To work in a Moscow brothel rather than in one of your seedier ones here? No, certainly not!" she replied sharply. "Besides, I thought you Russians regarded us German women as scum."

"I see, Fräulein, that you have a keen intellect and a sense of humour. The latter is unusual amongst Germans. Perhaps it is something you've picked up from your British lover," he retorted.

She felt their minds circling each other, his selecting the most vulnerable point to strike and hers calculating how best to parry his offers, accusations and threats.

"Why don't you come to the point? What is it that I have and you want?"

Kovalev did not reply, whether admiring her offensive strategy or angered by it she could not tell. He got up and stood behind her. She closed her eyes ready for the physical assault that would surely come. But it did not. She heard him open the door and give an order. He retook his seat opposite her but said nothing. He just smiled; none of Fortescue's subtlety. She heard the door shut. An older, rough-looking man in uniform came to the table, on which he placed her handbag. He glared at her as he did so. Kovalev waved him away. Looking at her, Kovalev opened the bag delicately and slowly tipped out its contents, spreading them across the table in front of him. In the middle was a black notebook. He picked it up and thumbed through the pages.

"It belongs to your British lover. I've glanced at it. There are no military secrets but some interesting personal information, particularly about you, about his movements over the past few days and his feelings towards you." He swivelled the notebook between his fingers. "But it's not the book we expected. We were more interested in another black notebook which, according to the one in my hand, you gave him in Munich after he rescued you. That's the book we want – badly. When we get it, your soldier friend can have his diary back. But there's something else we want as well and we think you can help us in our search."

Karin was frantically trying to collect her thoughts. In her haste to leave Fortescue without disturbing him, she had picked up the wrong book. Now she had exposed its contents and him to the Russians.

"Well, Fräulein Eilers, will you help us to get the real notebook and also do us the other favour?"

"What favour is that?" asked Karin, trying hard to stop her hand from trembling in fear of what it might be.

"We think your mother is still in Berlin – hiding from the victors, afraid to hand herself in and face the punishment for her misdeeds. The deal is this. You get us the book and tell us where your mother is and we'll let you go. If you don't, we will hold you until you change your mind. In those circumstances, you can forget about lipstick, mascara and pretty dresses. Life is hard for all those who cover up for the Nazis."

His finely manicured fingers gradually returned each item to her handbag, including Fortescue's notebook. She watched him, almost mesmerised by the precision and deftness of his hand.

"Well, Fräulein Eilers, do we have a deal?"

She had to play for time – to consider her options, just as she had once done in Frieda's flat when a repugnant SS *Standartenführer* had suggested a game of bondage. Now was the moment, as then, to become emotional, to display vulnerability. Tears welled in her eyes.

"I need time to think. I'm not sure which book you are talking about and I've had little to do with my mother in recent years. I abhor her."

"Don't play games with me, Fräulein. I believe you do know where she is. As for the book, no doubt your British lover has it. What's more important to him – the book or his thighs between yours?"

Karin could barely conceal her loathing for her interrogator. So different from the interrogation at Seeshaupt.

"You bastard," she replied, unable to contain her anger.

"Watch your tongue, woman. You Germans are all the same – arrogant, full of pride. But not any longer. We're the masters now. We, the victors, tell you, the vanquished, what to do."

He sprang up from the table and put his hand tightly around her throat as he pulled her to her feet.

"You have until this evening to reveal the whereabouts of what we want. If you don't, we'll convey you to the East to experience more generous Russian hospitality."

Taken along a corridor, she was pushed into a cell, the lock turned behind her. In the corner was a huddled figure, a middle-aged woman with a shaven head and bruised face, her dress filthy and torn.

"You don't have much time," the hunched figure whispered. "The penalties for holding out are beatings and sex."

Karin did not reply. Would this treatment be given to her mother? She slid to the floor, her head spinning.

* * * * *

Nolan sat behind his desk making notes as Fortescue recounted how Karin Eilers had made contact with him the day before and he had taken her to Wilmersdorf.

"Why didn't you inform me immediately after she had arrived at the hotel?"

"She was deeply upset. I decided to let her rest and to talk to her in the evening. By the time I returned from HQ, she was still sleeping. I sat with her through the night, intending to speak to her again this morning and convince her to stay. Once I had done so, I intended to speak to you. But I fell asleep. During that time, she got up and left – with a Russian, it would seem. Mrs Maddox saw the Russian vehicle drive off just as she arrived."

"Major Fortescue, you have been careless, to say the least. Ever since you arrived in Berlin, you've been skating on thin ice. Our patience is wearing equally thin. It would be even thinner, if it were the case that last night you had put your personal sexual gratification before duty to your country." He looked at Fortescue across the top of his rimless glasses. Fortescue did not respond. "And, moreover, I would suggest that you have not revealed all you know about Miss Eilers and have possibly withheld information about some of your own actions. Because you have done so, the position has become more delicate. The Russians, in breach of existing protocols, have come unannounced into the British sector and, without authorisation or explanation, removed someone who in our judgement had placed herself under our jurisdiction. That merits a protest to the Soviet authorities through the relevant channels. But that is unlikely to secure what we want, namely Miss Eilers and any information she may have about the fate of her mother."

Again, Fortescue did not reply. Though weighing the words of his pompous interrogator, his mind was more focused on the effect of his notebook. If the Russian security authorities had read its contents, it would place Karin in even greater danger and compromise him, providing the Russians with the opportunity for blackmail. The choice confronting him was stark: hand over the *Waffen* SS notebook, scrub Karin from his mind, board a plane to London with Susannah and put Germany behind him; or take a leaf from some of those he had interrogated at Nuremburg – say nothing of past misdeeds and tough it out. The first was the easier option, but his personal feelings for Karin – even though she had not said she reciprocated them – meant that he had to choose the second, despite the fact it might end in prosecution under the Official Secrets Act, possible imprisonment and the ruin of his reputation.

"I have nothing to add to what I've told you."

"So be it," said Nolan. "Wait outside."

Almost an hour later, Fortescue was summoned back to Nolan's room.

"I've arranged for Mrs Maddox to go to Karlshorst as soon as possible to complain about their unauthorised activity in the British sector yesterday. You should not go with her. Stay here in headquarters."

Fortescue made no comment, privately observing that Nolan had made no mention of seeking Karin's return.

* * * * *

That evening Fortescue and Dorothy met in the safe room at military headquarters. She sat opposite him across a green-baize-topped table and began by explaining the decision to send her to Karlshorst a courtesy pointedly omitted by Nolan himself; much of the background Fortescue already knew, but he appreciated her openness nonetheless.

Since the Kommandatura's foundation – following the entry of US and, subsequently, British forces into Berlin in July 1945, with the French on their coat-tails – the three Western Allies had been desperately trying to catch up with the consequences of Soviet sole occupation immediately following Russia's victorious entry into the city in May of that year. With the western sectors already stripped by the Russians of all remaining industrial and agricultural assets, the relationship between the four victorious wartime Allies was becoming increasingly fraught, as frequently reflected in the bad-tempered conduct of Kommandatura business at its headquarters in Dahlem, in the US sector. Given these circumstances, Dorothy explained, Nolan had decided that, in order to achieve his objectives, it would be best to approach the Russians low key and avoid the probability of the incident getting caught up in more formal Kommandatura business, which could defeat the object of his intentions. As she was currently in Berlin, and he had discovered she was a Russian speaker, he had selected her for the task in the hope that she might establish a rapport with whoever was her Soviet interlocutor.

"As it happens," Dorothy continued, "it appears that will be Colonel Valentin Sokolov. We got to know each other at Yalta when I was part of Churchill's support team. He's clever, amusing and sophisticated – a rare product from Stalin's machine. He struck me as highly perceptive and manipulative, a staunch defender of his country's interests. As a senior figure in the Ministry of State Security, he is a worthy opponent in the game of secrets – an accomplished card player. If I'm to outplay him, I want a good hand of cards. So, Major Fortescue, I want to see your cards – now. I want to know everything. If you want Miss Eilers back, I will have to play my hand well. I cannot do so if you hold back the truth. What is it to be?"

Fortescue looked at her. Should he tell her everything or be selective? If the latter, he would be spinning another web of half-truths and withholding more information. If the former, he would be placing his future and reputation in her hands. Or he could decline to respond as she had asked, board a plane and go back to London and marry Susannah. Or, yet again, he could risk everything for a woman he was unable to get out of his head.

"If I tell you all that I know, what will you do with it? Record it and hold it over me and then reveal it if I commit some indiscretion in the future? Or will you keep it safe and secure, known only to you?"

"I've no axe to grind, no ulterior motive," she replied. "I lost my husband early in marriage and to this day miss him greatly. My grief remains unassuaged – love by another name with nowhere to go, some say. It was evident to me in Munich – from what you said and how you glanced at her from time to time – that you had already fallen in love with Miss Eilers. If that is so, and she carries no wartime guilt, which I believe to be the case, I would like her and you to be united. Whatever happens thereafter is your affair. But to achieve this outcome, I need to know everything. If you feel you cannot trust me, I would understand your reluctance, and would advise you to leave Berlin as quickly as possible because there are people here who are jealous of your reputation and for that reason wish to pull you down. But if you trust me, then stay awhile – and confide in no one else."

Fortescue's mouth was dry. He took a sip of water from the glass in front of him and made his confession. He divulged the extent of his physical relationship with Karin, the two bodies he had seen in the flat she had shared with her friend Frieda, the man he had shot in Seeshaupt, and the deaths in Nuremburg of Herr Kellerman and the young prostitute. He revealed he had the black book, marked for Himmler's attention, which Karin had retrieved from the flat, and how Karin had intended to take it with her to East Berlin but instead had taken his notebook, his record of the past few days. As he spoke, Dorothy looked at him intently but without expression.

"Is that all?" she asked.

"Yes," he replied.

"And where is the black book now?"

"It's in my bag in the hotel."

"Who do you think told the Russians Karin was at the hotel?"

"I don't know."

"Did she disclose to you when you were together that they had contacted her?"

"No," he said firmly. "She just said she had to leave Berlin."

"Did she talk about her mother?"

"No. Only to tell me, in Seeshaupt, that she had got involved with the Nazi hierarchy and that in the last years of the war had lost contact with her."

"Thank you, Richard, for this information. You have put yourself in a delicate position and, if the Russians have your notebook, a potentially compromising one, which State Security will no doubt want to exploit. To get it back and secure Karin's release, we have to decide what to offer them in return." She paused. "Miss Eilers flew from Munich to Berlin, where on arrival she stayed in a place arranged by Major Steiner as a favour for you."

"Correct," said Fortescue.

"You then arranged for her to go to the hotel in Wilmersdorf. But before you could take her there she disappeared. There is no evidence of Soviet activity in that neighbourhood on that day. So where did she go for twenty-four hours? If she was not with you, or with Steiner, or the Russians, then who was she with? Are you sure she said nothing about her movements at that time?"

"All I can tell you is that she was distressed when she called on the phone, as though she was being pursued."

Dorothy got up and paced the room.

"I would like to see the SS notebook as quickly as possible. If it contains, as you have suggested, certain coded information for Himmler's personal attention, it is possible that its contents were of significant value to him in the closing stages of the war and, after his demise, of even greater value – perhaps monetary value – to those in the regime not yet apprehended, still trying to escape. If the book was hidden in the Munich flat, then Karin Eilers's mother may be the link – a direct connection between her and the *Reichsführer*."

Dorothy continued to pace the room, but no longer sharing her thoughts with Fortescue. He broke the silence.

"Is it not conceivable that ex-Nazis, involved in organising the escape of fugitives, abducted her from the accommodation in which Steiner had placed her, assuming she was in possession of the book – a book that might be the key to hidden money? Perhaps she even saw her mother. If that were the case, then what you could offer the Soviets is the prospect of us finding and handing over her mother in return for Karin and my book."

"That is an interesting supposition," replied Dorothy. "But finding her in order to prove your supposition will be hard. What I have to do is to probe Sokolov. If Miss Eilers's mother is to be the bait, then hard or not we do have to find her – assuming she is still in Berlin and has not fled abroad. And please, let me see the notebook. I think it may have great significance."

Fortescue did not respond.

* * * * *

It took an hour to reach Karlshorst, headquarters of the Soviet military administration in Germany.

Outwardly, Valentin Sokolov had changed little since Dorothy had last seen him. Still good-looking, he oozed smoothness, sleekness and self-confidence – the satisfied cat with cream on its whiskers. (She knew from their time together at Yalta that he thought of her as the quintessential English rose – delicate, fragrant, but with sharp thorns if not handled with care, he had elaborated, charmingly not quite grasping the meaning of the colloquialism he had chosen.) His uniform was well-cut and close-fitting. His proud demeanour bore all the familiar hallmarks of State Security. Though he was a good English speaker, they spoke in Russian as they sipped tea from the samovar. As with previous such sensitive, well-choreographed encounters in which she had taken part, where the vigilant interlocutors assess each other's strengths and weaknesses like fencers before the first thrust, they exchanged pleasantries – on this occasion, memories of Yalta, swapping impressions of a confident Stalin, a sick Roosevelt and a circumspect Churchill, three leaders, three master tacticians each with their own agenda. With the tea consumed, it was time to move to a closer engagement.

"How can I help my favourite English agent?" said Sokolov with a broad smile.

"Colonel, as I arrived at my hotel in Wilmersdorf a day or so ago, one of your vehicles pulled away." She passed him a slip of paper on which was written the vehicle's registration. "Inside was a young German woman. Your people did not seek prior approval for their visit. We would like to know why, and, of course, the whereabouts of the young woman in question – Karin Eilers."

"You've caught me unawares. I will have to check and get back to you."

"Colonel, don't play games. That is for others. You and I know we don't want to take this procedural matter to a higher level, for it to get out of hand. The Commandants have enough to discuss. I would like the two of us to get to the bottom of this and to find a solution. To do that, I would like to speak to her – either in your sector or ours. If she has useful information, we can share it to our mutual advantage. I would like this to happen as soon as possible."

Sokolov locked his fingers together. "My dear Dorothy, let's put formality aside, as we did before. I'll make some enquiries. That's all I can promise."

"Thank you, Valentin. Shall we meet again tomorrow and reach a suitable arrangement? After all, we co-operated one evening in Yalta, don't you remember? In an intimate moment, you were rather uncomplimentary about your General Secretary. We agreed afterwards that discretion was the better part of valour. If we were discreet then, why can't we be discreet now?"

He did not reply.

She smiled at him. "Come, Valentin, we can solve this little misunderstanding. It's what we are good at."

"We'll see, dear Dorothy, we'll see."

They shook hands.

That evening, she received a message inviting her to return to Karlshorst the following morning to see the prisoner, Fräulein Eilers.

On arrival, Dorothy was received not by Valentin Sokolov but by Major Kovalev, whom she remembered as a peripheral presence at Yalta and who now escorted her to a windowless upstairs room. Karin was already seated at the rough-hewn table. Dorothy sat opposite her, struck by the young woman's composure. Physically striking, her face was pale and drawn, framed by thick dark shoulder-length hair; she wore little make-up. Despite her outward calmness, her eyes could not hide the fear of her predicament.

Kovalev was about to sit down beside Dorothy but she brushed him away.

"Major, this discussion is à deux. Your presence is not required."

Kovalev started to protest but Dorothy stopped him.

"This was agreed with Colonel Sokolov. Shall we call him to confirm his instruction?"

Muttering his evident displeasure, Kovalev left the room.

Indicating with a silent gesture that the room was bugged, Dorothy began the conversation.

"Would you like a cigarette?"

Karin nodded. With slender fingers she eased one from the silver case Dorothy proffered. Her hand revealed a slight tremble as she leaned towards the strong flame of Dorothy's lighter.

"Are they treating you well?"

"Yes," replied Karin, unconvincingly. Invited to say more she described guardedly, briefly – Dorothy requiring few words to understand the true picture – that she had been interviewed, then held in a cell until the previous evening, when she had been taken to a room upstairs. Though it was spartan, and the door had been locked behind her, she'd had a more comfortable night's sleep. And her handbag had been returned to her; the contents were all there, with one exception – which Dorothy noted with the slightest of nods.

"Did you come here of your own free will or were you brought here under duress?"

"I received an invitation – an invitation I evidently could not refuse – to discuss how I might be able to help with some enquiries they are making."

"Help in what way?"

"To tell them what might have happened to my mother."

"What did you say?"

"I said, as I have done to others, that I could not help. That my mother disappeared from my life well before the end of the war."

The exchange paused.

"What price do you place on loyalty?" asked Dorothy.

"Loyalty to whom? I owe loyalty to no one," Karin retorted.

"I meant loyalty to one's family, loyalty to one's ideals," said Dorothy.

"Germany is crushed. The Nazis led us into the abyss. Those who are left face a struggle simply to exist. There is no room for ideals. I just want to survive, to be left alone."

"And what about your family? What of them?"

"My father was killed long ago by the movement he supported. My brother was recently murdered in Munich."

"And what about your mother? How do you regard her?"

"I loved her once, but she became intoxicated by Nazi ideology, by being close to its principal exponents. We drifted apart."

"Tell me about her," said Dorothy.

As Karin gave her ritual answer, Dorothy took a slip of paper from her bag and wrote on it. Ensuring that the conversation continued, she pushed the slip across the table. On it was the question: Do you know where she is now? Karin read it. Almost imperceptibly she nodded. As their talk moved to life in Munich in the last months of the war, Dorothy wrote another question on the reverse of the slip of paper: Where? Karin mouthed the reply "Berlin". Could you show me whereabouts on a map? wrote Dorothy. Again Karin nodded.

The conversation carried on for several more minutes, over another cigarette.

"Thank you, Miss Eilers, for your co-operation. I will return soon."

"I hope so," whispered Karin. "This is a place of darkness."

As Dorothy waited on the steps for her car, she was joined by Sokolov. She turned to him.

"Let her go. If you don't and anything happens to her, I will be your enemy."

Sokolov said nothing.

In the early hours of the next morning, Dorothy received an urgent message from Sokolov asking her to return to Karlshorst as soon as possible. When she arrived at the military base he took her immediately to a cell block. In cell number 9 was Karin, sitting on the floor hugging her knees. Her wrists were handcuffed, her dress crumpled and blood-spattered. The guard ordered her to stand to attention.

"What happened, Colonel?" Dorothy asked in a cold, matter-of-fact voice.

Before he could answer, Karin shouted, "That filthy pig of a Major tried to rape me. I hope the bastard dies."

Dorothy helped Karin to the bench at the back of the cell.

"I moved her to this more secure room in the women's wing where I could keep a closer eye on her," said Sokolov, "but Major Kovalev ignored instructions and came to see her. She claims he tried to rape her. He says she tried to escape. In the struggle a shot was fired from his pistol."

"How is Kovalev?"

"They think he will survive. But once he is strong enough there will have to be a trial to establish the truth – attempted escape or attempted rape. She will have to stay."

"Who will protect her in the meantime?"

"I will make the necessary arrangements," replied Sokolov.

"I would like a few minutes alone with her."

"You keep pushing me. You have ten minutes. The guard will be outside. Ten minutes – that is all you have."

There was little conversation. Karin was a mixture of despair and defiance, enveloped in shock. She rocked back and forth on the bench.

"I'm going mad – lost in a dark endless forest. There is no way out."

"There is," Dorothy assured her. "Tell me where your mother is. If we can find her, this nightmare can end."

"I would not wish this hell on anyone – even her."

Dorothy did her best to comfort Karin but to no avail.

"When I die, I will become a vengeful fury from beyond the grave. I will show no mercy to those who have done this to me. Everyone has betrayed me."

"Major Fortescue did not betray you. He cares for you. He wants you back. I will do everything I can – with him – to make that possible. Don't despair. Hold on."

The guard unlocked the cell door to announce that their time was up.

Sokolov escorted Dorothy to her vehicle.

"Save her, Valentin, save her. She's an innocent young woman, a victim of the fallout of this terrible war. There has been enough suffering. Let her go."

"My dear friend, if only it were that easy. I will do my best to protect her. But she will have to stand trial for the attempted murder of a Soviet officer. The military prosecutor will insist on that. Let us hope for her sake that the truth prevails."

"And if it does not?" replied Dorothy. "You may not win the prize you have long sought."

"And what is that?"

"You do not need me to tell you."

CHAPTER EIGHT

Nightmare

At the best of times the city offered bleak prospects – dismal skies by day and chilling darkness after dusk. At the worst of times, the unrelenting bitterness of the wind and the consequent dulling of the senses made it an uncompromising foe of endurance and the resilience of the human spirit. Winter had now assaulted Berlin. As each day passed it steadily strengthened its iron grip, highlighting the breadth and depth of the city's destruction and the miserable existence of its inhabitants, while the victors continued to squabble over the application and demarcation of their rights. It had become an unforgiving time. In different parts of the divided capital of defeated Germany three people – Karin Eilers, her mother and Richard Fortescue – woke to face another day.

* * * * *

In what she now knew – only too well – to be a dilapidated, partially destroyed and unheated former munitions factory on the eastern edge of the city's Russian sector, Karin stirred as the prison guards urged their charges to their feet. After washing in icy water, lining up for the roll-call in her filthy rough shirt, coarse trousers and open sandals, and drinking some lukewarm greasy soup for breakfast, she began another day of her survival – monotonous labour to the strains of rousing Communist songs designed to inspire the masses. The only breaks she had from this routine were the periodic visits of Dorothy Maddox, but they were short and without privacy. Despite the constant surveillance of the guards, Dorothy was able to hand over small items that could be hidden. On one occasion, she produced some hairgrips so Karin could pin her hair up in the hope of avoiding another brutal shearing. On another, she gave her the last twists of some lipstick, which enabled her to barter a margin of friendship with one particular prison guard – a smear of lipstick in return for being spared the bullying tactics and searches of her rudimentary bed, where she secreted Dorothy's latest delivery. The greatest danger was at night, after the few lights in the prison had been extinguished: the visits from male prison guards, drawn from the army, seeking sexual gratification. Tightly wrapped in her dirty iron-grey blanket, Karin had already repelled three attempts to rape her, despite Sokolov's earlier promise to protect her.

A week later, Karin received news from Dorothy that she was to be tried in five days' time for the attempted murder of Major Ivan Kovalev. She showed little emotion at the news. She had been expecting it.

"Thank you for telling me. It will be good to know my fate. I'm under no illusion as to the outcome."

"You must be brave," said Dorothy, reaching out to clasp her hand.

Karin smiled.

"Death will come as a relief from this misery," she replied.

"A guilty verdict is not a foregone conclusion," insisted Dorothy. "You must speak up in your defence. I intend to be present at the proceedings."

"Thank you," said Karin.

"Five minutes left," shouted the warder.

"I have brought you a book to read." Dorothy pushed a well-used copy of Goethe's *Italian Journey* across the table.

"Thank you," said Karin. "There is little opportunity to read but it's kind of you to think of me."

"It's not from me. It's from Major Fortescue. He has written inside it."

Karin opened the book. In bold decisive handwriting, he had written:

To Karin
As you run your fingers over Goethe's words, close your eyes
and let the touch of the print weave magic as you journey in
your imagination. From your companion, RF

Closing the book, she leaned across the table. "All the things I once thought unimaginable – even in war – exist in this dreadful place of demons. They come during the night to take me to interrogation. The same procedure, the same system but at unpredictable times, trying to break my spirit. I will do my best not to give in, but if the worst happens I have hidden a length of cord which I will use to hang myself – it is for me to end my life, not them."

"Karin, I urge you not to give in, not to give up. This will all surely end in your favour. And when it does, Major Fortescue intends to be there to help you, should that be your wish."

Karin tried to keep the emotion from her face as she felt a flicker of comfort at the mention of his name.

"Time up," shouted the guard.

Dorothy clasped her hand, promising to have a further conversation with Colonel Sokolov about guaranteeing her protection.

As Karin retraced her footsteps to her cell, jostled by the chief warder, the vast empty halls of the prison echoed to the sound of hideous music and occasional screams. With the music came the pungent stench of fear. Despite Dorothy and Colonel Sokolov, she feared for her safety in this Hades. That night a Soviet prison guard again attempted to rape her. Again, Karin repelled her attacker, helped by the female warder, to whom she gave the remaining stub of lipstick in gratitude.

* * * * *

On the western edge of the city, Helga Eilers stumbled out of her creaking truckle bed. Her physical condition was rapidly deteriorating in the damp basement of the house to which she had confined herself since her escape from Hitler's bunker. It required increasing willpower to stir each day – to throw the musty blankets back and get up. This morning she had woken much earlier than usual. Unable to return to sleep, she recalled yet again her memories of her days in the Minister's outer office, the frequent receptions at the Reich Chancellery, her first visit to the Berghof and tea in the Eagle's Nest. She recalled the elegant silk dresses she had worn and the sexual favours she had willingly granted to pay for them. She had been close to power, sensed its glow, seen its exercise, and at times, in bed with a lover, his uniform slung across a chair, had felt an intimate part of it. It had become a drug, an aphrodisiac. Being with the generals and close to the inner circle around Eva Braun had swelled her vanity and hubris. The deaths of others, the fate of Nazi victims – about which she had heard countless rumours, which made them true for many – were all swept aside by her pleasure, her thrill, at being ever closer to the core of the Reich.

She recalled vividly Hitler's speech to the Reichstag in January 1941 – at which she had been present – when to thunderous applause he had celebrated the indomitable spirit of the German people and their unwavering commitment to his leadership. His words, his passion, had inspired her to even greater effort and sacrifice in her work. Oh, what heady days they were! He had seemed invincible. Even after the enemy bombing of Berlin had begun, she had still believed in his reassurance that the destruction inflicted on the city was the price that had to be paid for the eventual vanquishing of the Reich's enemies – a belief to which she, like others, had clung almost to the end.

Gradually the dark shadows had lengthened and she had been increasingly aware that the *bon vivant*, happy-go-lucky attitudes of those around the Führer were becoming more sombre as they began to contemplate a different outcome. Towards the end, it was only the SS and Goebbels and his ilk who remained convinced that a final victory could still be achieved – once all the obstacles in its way had been removed.

She too had tried to remain optimistic, but before long the possibility of losing the war began to enter her mind as well. As defeat followed defeat early in 1945 in the East, friends urged her to leave Berlin before it was too late. But she stayed steadfastly loyal, proud to be part of the diminishing clique around Hitler. As the circle got ever smaller, increasing proximity to him inflamed her ardour for the cause, renewing her belief that defeat would turn into victory. Once it became evident the Goebbels family and her beloved leader intended to commit suicide, however, she had finally decided to flee, to join others who had escaped, in order to keep the national socialist flame alive, even though she really knew it was a lost cause.

A deeper, stronger motive for her eventual flight had been to avoid falling into Russian hands – an unimaginable fate. She had left the bunker by night, shown the way by a young army liaison officer who had also decided to leave and to try to break through the encircling Soviet lines, in order to find his family to the south of Berlin. He had taken her to a house in Kreuzberg where she met Helmut Fuchs, formerly of the Gestapo. Together with Helmut's sister, Gretchen, a strong Party sympathiser, they had reached the "safe" house in Grunewald, once owned by a Jewish family – the Feldmanns – but expropriated by the SS for so-called weekend recreational purposes. In the rooms on the first and second floors were two families, once staunch Party supporters, with their own deeds to hide, who had fled the Russian advance in the East. She, Helmut and Gretchen, living in the basement flat, had spun the story that they too had been misplaced. But this slender bond of apparent shared experience did little to encourage daily conversation. Accordingly, there was little social contact between the different floors of the house, each group being wary of the others, each aware of the possibility that the house might be reclaimed; and even more acutely aware that the Allies might come knocking at the door to check identity papers.

Some eighteen months later the world Helga Eilers had once enjoyed had long gone. The trappings of power – the dresses, the jewellery and the parties – were a distant, fading memory. Her daughter was in Russian hands; the documentation she had sought to preserve as insurance for her future had vanished; and she had concluded she could not rely for much longer on the loyalty of the handful of people supposed to be around her, allegedly working in her and Helmut's interest but hardly ever spoken of and never seen. Abandoning her self-delusion, she came to the conclusion that these people had probably never existed. Or, if they did, she was not important enough to qualify for the help they might be providing. Moreover, there was no mutual affection between her and Helmut. They were simply bound by the common bond of self-preservation. The newspaper reports of the outcome of the Nuremburg trial and the subsequent trials of those lower down the chain of command were a regular reminder of what fate might await them.

Helmut, she knew, had tortured several people to death in Gestapo headquarters in Prinz-Albrecht-Straße in the 1930s and had largely remained there during its many changes, including in 1939 when it became the Reich Main Security Office under the command of Reinhard Heydrich. He realised that, if he were apprehended, he would certainly face trial and the prospect of execution if found guilty. As for Helga herself, she had amongst her sins of commission, as her accusers would see it, denounced two Jewish families who had subsequently been transported to the East. That apart, her main guilt lay in her close involvement with the Party hierarchy. The sentence for her would be de-Nazification at best and a prison term at worst.

After dressing in her familiar slacks and jumper, she sat beside the cheerless fire to reflect on her options yet again. She could stay in the cellar until the spring, in the increasingly forlorn hope that her and Helmut's earlier discreet enquiries about the so-called "escape line" might result in the previously vaunted assistance, or just leave and seek to blend into a local community far away from Berlin under an assumed name. Her daughter would never come looking for her and her son was dead. But as had happened innumerable times before, she remained indecisive. She would wait one more week.

An hour or so later Helmut and Gretchen came to tell her that they were going out to get some fresh air and to buy some bread. To her surprise they did not return. At lunchtime, the elderly woman on the first floor, Frau Krause, came downstairs to report that she had heard from the next-door neighbour that Herr Fuchs had fallen in the snow and suffered a heart attack. A passer-by had stopped and called for help. A military vehicle had taken him and Gretchen to hospital. That evening Frau Krause visited again, to say that she understood Herr Fuchs remained unconscious and had been placed under guard at the hospital as his face had apparently been recognised from a list of wanted Gestapo personnel. His sister had mysteriously disappeared. Helga's mind was in turmoil. She had to leave immediately. If Helmut recovered consciousness and divulged where he had been living, she faced the prospect of arrest. What she had feared most now seemed about to unfold. She would have to leave Berlin alone and quickly. Her so-called friends had either been arrested or had deserted the cause.

She took down a small scruffy brown case from the shelf behind the curtain and filled it with a change of clothes. Underneath, she placed two small framed pictures wrapped in brown paper, one of Goebbels and the other of Hitler. Wrapped separately was her diamond swastika pendant and her ring. It was a huge risk, taking them with her, but if ever she needed money desperately they might fetch a good price from souvenir hunters on the black market. Also on the shelf was a shoebox in which was a moderate sum of Reichsmarks she had managed to keep hidden from Fuchs and his sister. Inside the box too was her identity card, reissued to her in 1943. The picture showed the face of an attractive and confident bureaucrat, so different from the grey-haired care-worn woman putting on her boots, a shabby thick black coat, an old fur hat and gloves. Putting the identity card in her handbag together with the cyanide phial she had been given in the bunker, she took one last look at the cellar, switched off the light and climbed the creaking staircase to the ground floor. She paused to listen for anyone on the landings above. There was silence. She tiptoed to the front door and stepped out into the cold, her boots crunching on the crisp snow. She walked slowly towards the S-Bahn station, eyes down but her ears vigilant for the sound of anyone behind her. At the station, she found by chance a taxi discharging a passenger. She asked the driver to take her to a small guest house in Spandau that Helmut had told her about – a basic room where he said no questions would be asked. There she would spend the night and decide where to go to next and how she would do so.

* * * * *

Some three hours before, Gretchen had returned to the hospital out of loyalty to her brother. There she had been questioned, confirming her brother's identity and disclosing the address in Grunewald where they had been living, sharing rooms with a Frau Eilers, who had once worked for Herr Goebbels. Later, military police arrived at the house in Grunewald, not long after Helga had left. They found no one downstairs but in the fireplace in a side room they found the smouldering remains of a swastika flag. Though the upstairs neighbours were able to provide little additional information, their description of the woman who lived in the cellar tallied with that given by Gretchen Fuchs. This was sufficient for the police to state in their report their belief that Frau Helga Eilers, formerly on the staff of Joseph Goebbels, was apparently alive and should be urgently sought for questioning. A warrant was issued the next morning for her arrest.

* * * * *

That very morning Richard Fortescue went to British military headquarters where he had a temporary job as a translator and language teacher to young army staff just arrived from London. He knew this work would not last for long. He would soon have to return to England to decide his future, including marriage to Susannah. But he could not banish Karin Eilers from his mind. He was determined to wait for the outcome of her trial. If she were found not guilty and released, he wanted her to be with him, provided that was what she too wanted after her ordeal. If she were convicted and sentenced to death or to a long prison term in a Soviet labour camp, he would be powerless. He would have to leave Germany and leave behind the woman with whom he had fallen in love. In those circumstances, he could not bear the thought of being locked in marriage to a woman he could never love. Susannah wrote to him regularly but her letters began to adopt a more uncompromising tone – unless he was back in London by the end of February she would ask her father to issue an order for his compulsory return. After all, she had written, it was cruel of a man she loved so much to treat her and her family in such a cavalier and uncaring way. It was a situation he could not allow to fester for much longer. Before leaving his billet, he checked that the black book was still secure in its hiding place. He decided that in the evening he would try once again to decipher its code.

On arrival at his desk in Lancaster House he found a message to go and see Charles Nolan immediately. Nolan was stiff and unfriendly; nothing unusual in that.

"Earlier this morning I received a message through our liaison with the Americans that a Munich detective called Hessler is on his way to Berlin to talk to you about the death – or rather, suspected murder – of a man in a place called Seeshaupt. It's near Munich. Looking at my notes, I see that was the place where you stayed overnight with Fräulein Eilers."

"Why does he wish to see me?" asked Fortescue, trying to appear nonchalant.

"Because," replied Nolan, "an innkeeper gave a description of a couple that appeared to fit the two of you. Moreover, both the innkeeper and a boatman they also questioned thought you might be in the military because of your demeanour."

"I don't think I have any information to give him. Yes, she and I were in Seeshaupt, and I recall the boatman and the innkeeper. But that is all."

"In the interests of building the trust of the local police and to keep our American friends happy, I've agreed to the detective's request. He wishes to interview you as soon as he arrives."

"And what does my commanding officer have to say?" asked Fortescue.

"He agrees. So please stay at your desk to await his arrival. Discuss this matter with no one."

Fortescue got up but before leaving the room asked Nolan if he had any further information about Karin.

"None," replied Nolan curtly. "Mrs Maddox goes to Karlshorst from time to time but she is now doing so on separate instructions from London. I have advised her that the young woman is likely to be found guilty and, if so, possibly executed – one less German to worry about, if I may put it crudely. I think Mrs Maddox is of the same opinion. If I am right, the case will soon be closed, and your assistance in the matter will no longer be required. By the way, Mrs Maddox has had to fly to London to see her sick father. She hopes to be back in the next few days. Until then, Major Fortescue, it is just you, me and Inspector Hessler."

Fortescue did not return to his desk. Instead, he stepped outside to smoke a cigarette. He was puzzled that after all this time a detective from Munich should come to Berlin out of the blue to interview him about a man he had shot in self-defence, a fact that he had stupidly not disclosed under earlier questioning from Nolan, to avoid admitting that he had fired his pistol while off duty. What was equally worrying, indeed more so, was that he could not remember whether he had disclosed the incident in his notebook, now in Russian hands and which might be reproduced in evidence at Karin's trial. He paced up and down the yard. He was in a bind of his own making. After more pacing, he knew he had little choice but to give Hessler his side of the story. But exactly how much he divulged would depend on what Hessler asked him. Though the German police still had little credibility, it was nonetheless possible that he might eventually have to face the possibility of arrest for murder. The only witness was in Russian hands. Moreover, there was also the incident with Kellerman in Nuremburg. Might Hessler ask him about that and indeed about the murder of Frieda and Gerhard? He sensed that the ground beneath his feet becoming unstable.

CHAPTER NINE

False Tranquillity

Max Steiner's information was correct. Detective Hessler was a tall, well-built man in his early forties. Born and bred in Munich, he had served in the city police department during the Nazi regime but despite loyalty to his superiors no promotion had come his way, partly, it seemed, because he had fallen foul of the local Gestapo for insubordination and failure to follow instructions. Thereafter, he had been given mundane duties. After interrogation at the end of the war and various checks by the US authorities, it had been decided Hessler was largely untainted by the past, despite his Party membership, which he claimed had been compulsory. He was therefore reappointed to the police force and promised promotion in due course – provided he performed well and showed no favours to former colleagues who had more to answer for their actions.

As they exchanged pleasantries across a bare table, there was something about Hessler that put Fortescue on his guard. His mannerisms – the fastidious way in which he positioned his glasses on the table, his well-manicured fingernails, the occasional hint of humour and the cultivated air of childlike innocence – reminded him of the habits of some of the accused he had interviewed in Nuremburg. Many of those convicted had displayed a similar façade of urbanity. Fortescue struggled to hide his irritation at being questioned by a German detective to whom he had taken an early dislike, a police officer who just a year or so ago had probably raised his arm daily in the Nazi salute. He wondered precisely how much Hessler had known about Nazi atrocities. Had he been one of the thousands of petty officials who had turned a blind eye? After all, Dachau had been just down the road from Munich. Hessler interrupted his thoughts.

"Shall we begin, Major Fortescue?"

Fortescue nodded. It was agreed that the conversation would be in German. Before Hessler could begin, his opponent in the game now about to be played made the first move.

"On what basis is our conversation?" asked Fortescue. "If it is formal, I should like the presence of a witness – for obvious reasons I am sure you will appreciate."

Hessler smiled and offered Fortescue a cigarette, which he declined.

"This is an informal conversation, a chat, off the record, as a journalist might say. I will make a few notes. That is all. What might happen later is a matter of pure conjecture," he added.

Fortescue detected a barely repressed smile of self-satisfaction.

"I too will make notes, to ensure we conduct our conversation on an equal footing."

Hessler nodded his agreement. Both men looked at each other, sizing each other up. Fortescue assumed from the start that someone would eavesdrop on what was said – the bookshelf close to the interview table was an obvious place to hide a microphone – though whether friend or enemy, he could not say; perhaps both. Charles Nolan was top of his list of candidates.

The game continued.

"My colleagues and I are seeking information about the death of a man, Franz Zimmermann, whose body was found some weeks ago in the forest above Seeshaupt, a small town –"

"I know the place," interrupted Fortescue.

"Because," Hessler continued, "according to the innkeeper near the quay, you visited Seeshaupt around the time of Zimmermann's murder. He was precise about it."

"I'm sure he was. Yes, I was there – with Fräulein Karin Eilers. We had gone to Seeshaupt to get away from the city before I left for Berlin. We stayed at the inn for a short while before returning to Munich."

"Did you stay in the inn the whole time or did you go out? For a walk along the lake, perhaps, or in the forest."

"Why do you ask?"

"I just want to know if you saw or heard anything suspicious."

"We went for a walk but returned soon after to get warm. We were lovers, you see."

"After such a short time?" Hessler replied, feigning surprise.

"Yes. We were attracted to one another. For that reason, there was no point staying out in the cold. Bed had more to offer than a walk."

"Did you see anyone acting suspiciously while you were in Seeshaupt?"

"No," replied Fortescue, already inwardly justifying his decision not to disclose that he had been in the forest and shot Zimmermann – if that was his name. After all, Hessler had not placed him under formal questioning. Besides, he was not going to reveal what had happened while Karin was still in Russian hands. The Soviets might have informants in the Munich police department and any confession on his part might be used in evidence against her, as proof that she had already been involved in murder.

Evidently seeing that his early line of questioning was yielding few results, Hessler tried other approaches to probe for inconsistencies in Fortescue's answers. But Fortescue's sharp legal skill and interviewing technique, honed at the Nuremburg tribunal, enabled him to avoid the traps his opponent was seeking to set. He took out a cigarette and slowly lit it, waiting for the next inevitable question. But it was not the one he expected.

"Two murders took place in Nuremburg while you were in the city following Fräulein Eilers's departure for Berlin."

"You seem well informed about my movements. How is that, may I ask?"

"We liaise with our colleagues in Nuremburg to see if there are any patterns in criminal activities between the two cities. And we are being well trained under the new regime – to look for connections, similarities, recurring features in the commission of crimes. Moreover, we like of course to ensure the personal safety of the occupying powers."

"So I see," replied Fortescue.

He decided to throw some bait to Hessler.

"While I was at the Nuremburg courthouse for a few days on official business, I spent an evening with a British security colleague, whose name I can provide if necessary. We had a few drinks in a bar. Afterwards, I decided to walk back to where I was staying, to see whether any progress had been made in rebuilding."

"The city that you the Allies demolished," interjected Hessler.

Fortescue ignored the interruption. "In the square near the executioner's house I was approached by a man who gave his name as Kellerman. He said he was a policeman and wanted me to go to the Sebaldus church – a church that incidentally I had admired architecturally before the war. He said I might find someone of interest there with information for the tribunal."

"But the tribunal is over."

"Indeed it is, but there are always some loose ends. I was interested in one of those."

"How did this man know you?" interrupted Hessler.

"I've no idea," replied Fortescue.

"That's odd, to say the least."

Fortescue continued.

"On the way, I was accosted by a young woman who asked for money in return for sex. I declined and urged her to go home as the streets were unsafe. I went to the church as Kellerman suggested but saw no one – that is to say, I recognised no one there and no one approached me. I left and went to my lodging."

"When did you hear of the two murders?"

"My British security friend told me the following morning."

"Nothing else?" enquired Hessler.

He looked at Fortescue, who shook his head. For his part he was almost enjoying deflecting the detective's efforts. He wondered whether Hessler had been forewarned about his background, that he was a skilful manipulator of questions both as interviewer and interviewee. Finding a chink in his defence was clearly proving difficult. Obviously concluding that further questions about Kellerman and the young prostitute would serve little purpose – for now at least – Hessler tried another tactic. Once again he offered Fortescue a cigarette. This time he accepted.

"Fräulein Eilers shared an apartment near the *Hauptbahnhof* in Munich with a young woman and a man believed to be her brother. They were brutally murdered around the time you met the Fräulein – we believe it was on the day you and she went to the opera. We have an eyewitness account – from a taxi driver – that you went with her to the apartment late in the evening and that shortly thereafter you both left again in a hurry. Why was that?"

Fortescue sat back, adopting an air of calm.

"Fräulein Eilers accepted my offer to accompany her back to the flat after we had been to the opera. Indeed, I insisted that I do so. As a young unmarried woman, she, like many others in Germany, is at risk from predators. On arrival at her apartment block, she got out of the taxi. I went with her to the main entrance where we said goodnight. I paused for a moment to ensure she reached the floor – the third – where she said she lived. I was turning away when I heard her scream. I ran upstairs where a man in a dark coat and hat was attempting to rape her. I punched him a couple of times. He fell and I pulled Fräulein Eilers downstairs to safety. We took the taxi in which we had come back to my accommodation, where I reported her presence to a British officer."

"How do you know the man was trying to rape her? After all, it was dark."

"I used my lighter to see as I ran upstairs. His left hand had her pinned against the wall by her throat and the right was up her skirt."

"Did you go into the apartment, Major Fortescue?"

"No. I did not."

"Did you and the Fräulein go back to the apartment the following day?"

Fortescue thought quickly, whether to say yes or no.

"Yes. I took her back by taxi so she could collect some fresh clothes. She was still upset by what had happened the night before."

"Did you accompany her upstairs?"

"Yes."

"Did you enter the flat?"

"Yes."

"What did you see?"

"It was an indescribable scene. I quickly took Fräulein Eilers away. She was distraught."

"How long do you think you were there?"

"Six or seven minutes – no more than that."

"Hmm," murmured Hessler. "Another eyewitness we have – the taxi driver who took you to the apartment that day and whom you asked to wait – suggested that you and Fräulein Eilers were in the building for some fifteen minutes or more."

Fortescue inwardly cursed his stupidity at forgetting the taxi driver.

"What were you doing during that time? The Fräulein left without taking any fresh clothes, to use your phrase. The taxi driver said she got out of his cab with only a handbag and returned with just the handbag, which appeared to leave a small bloodstain on the seat. And he noticed a damp-looking mark or stain on her coat. So, what were you doing, if she did not find any clothes?"

Finding it hard to restrain his temper, Fortescue said the Fräulein had collapsed on the bloodstained floor at the sight of the two bodies. That no doubt accounted for the stain on her coat and the blood on her handbag. He had brought her round and then persuaded her to leave – without collecting any clothes.

"I've just a couple more questions, Major, if I may."

"Yes, Detective, what are they?"

"A neighbour on the floor above has told us she heard a

woman's voice that morning, shouting repeatedly, 'I must find the book.' If the witness is correct – as we believe she is – what was the book the Fräulein was looking for? Did she find it? And if she did, where is it now?"

Fortescue's mouth became dryer. Hessler was no pushover after all.

"Miss Eilers did find a black notebook, beneath a floorboard. She put it in her handbag. The bag and its contents are now with her – in Russian hands."

"Did you ever look inside the book?"

"Yes, once. It was in some kind of code. I could not decipher it as I am not a code-breaker."

Hessler made no comment. He then sprang his last question.

"The neighbour above said she saw you leave the flat putting a hand gun into your coat pocket. We know you had no part in the killing of the two occupants because they were tortured and died a slow and brutal death, much longer than the fifteen minutes you and Fräulein Eilers were in the apartment. But my question is this: Did you have your gun with you at Seeshaupt?"

"Yes," replied Fortescue. "I always carry a gun for the purpose of self-defence, in accordance with British military regulations."

"Even when off duty, out of uniform?" queried Hessler.

"It depends on the circumstances," said Fortescue.

"That is all, Major," said Hessler, putting his notebook back in his pocket and replacing his glasses in their case. "Thank you for being so helpful. That has cleared up a number of matters. It's a pity Fräulein Eilers is not available, but we cannot have everything in these difficult times."

Fortescue accompanied Hessler to his car, parked on the Platz outside Lancaster House. They shook hands and the detective drove off. As Fortescue slowly walked back to the headquarters building, he had to acknowledge that the policeman had proved a worthy opponent – persistent, agile and remarkably well-informed. But two things struck him.

First, Hessler had not asked whether he had fired his pistol in Seeshaupt. Why had he not done so? Second, not all of the information Hessler had divulged had come from just five eyewitnesses – an innkeeper, a boatman, two taxi drivers and a neighbour on the floor above Frieda's flat. It seemed to him that Hessler had possibly had access to another source. Who could that be? Was it Dorothy, in whom he had confided most? Had she betrayed his confidence and now placed herself out of reach in London? Or was it someone else? Whatever the source, it had been an even contest of wits across the table.

He was suddenly distracted by the noise of low-flying aircraft. He looked up and as he did so he caught sight of Nolan peering at him through a first-floor window.

Little of note happened for the rest of the day. In the early evening, Fortescue and Steiner met for a drink. Later that night, Fortescue took the small black book from its hiding place and sat down to try to decipher its contents over a whisky or two. There were plenty of experts he could consult – in Berlin, interception and decryption was done on an extensive scale. But this book was too precious to disclose. The only person who knew he had it was Dorothy, who had flown to London at short notice on undisclosed business; he didn't for one minute believe she was seeing a sick father. If he could not unpick the code, he would ask for her help – provided she returned soon and was able to convince him that she had not betrayed his confidence. But the book would have to stay in his possession. After all, it was Karin's and if he could break the code its value might be enhanced and it might carry greater weight in trying to secure her release, though how that would be done was hard to imagine. As Fortescue pored over the book, another letter from Susannah remained unopened.

He abandoned his efforts around midnight. Unsettled by Hessler's questioning, and anticipating possible further, formal action against him, he secreted the black book where it would not be found if, as he suspected, the RMPs were ordered to search his room. He crossed his fingers that Dorothy Maddox would return soon to give him advice.

* * * * *

In preparation for an expected instruction from London, Charles Nolan prepared a request to the British Commandant for permission to begin the formal questioning of Major Richard Fortescue, in the presence of military police officers, concerning the alleged commission of certain offences relevant to Britain's national security. The request was granted.

* * * * *

The following morning, Fortescue was summoned to Nolan's office to be told that Hessler wished to ask him some further questions, to clarify answers he had given the day before.

Two hours later, the questioning resumed. Fortescue was aware that the detective had spent almost half an hour with Nolan beforehand, and was ever more vigilant of the traps that, from their collusion, might have been set for him. When Hessler terminated the interview after an hour of persistent questions, Fortescue felt confident that he had evaded his efforts to ensnare his quarry.

* * * * *

Nolan, who had indeed been listening, concluded that the planned further action was the only way forward.

As the questioning ended, Helga Eilers prepared to leave her hotel to seek a new life under an assumed name.

CHAPTER TEN

Betrayal

On the afternoon of Monday 27 January 1947 – the day Detective Hessler questioned Fortescue for the second time – five people sat around a stained and scratched oak table in London. Four were men. The fifth was Dorothy Maddox. Outside number 54 Broadway, headquarters of Britain's counter-intelligence service, more snow was falling from a low leaden sky. It was bitterly cold – the beginning, though few realised it, of a long, unremitting and cruel winter that would bring profound hardship to the people of Britain after the rigours of the war. It was a meeting to review the increasingly intensive Soviet espionage activities in Berlin's western sectors and the effectiveness of existing counter-measures. A sixth seat was empty, awaiting the arrival of the head of MI6's counter-espionage section R5. Harold Adrian Russell Philby was preoccupied with other business but had said in his message excusing his absence that he would join the meeting as soon as he was free.

The head of the service, the taciturn Stewart Menzies, spoke first.

"I've asked Mrs Maddox, currently on assignment in Berlin, to brief us on some information that has recently come to light in the city. Mrs Maddox, please tell us the latest position."

The three other men around the table looked at Dorothy with barely hidden contempt. To them, she was out of place, out of her depth. While women may have been numerous in the wartime SOE and at Bletchley Park, the business of foiling Russian intelligence and other enemies of the realm was a man's job, done by men educated at public school and alumni of Oxford and Cambridge. In their opinion, she should be sitting at a typewriter or fetching tea. Well-used to the male chauvinism of her so-called colleagues, but frequently finding it difficult to conceal her disdain for them, she had prepared her short update well in advance – just enough information to catch their attention, while withholding the details of her dossier which she would divulge at a later date if the plan taking place in her mind were to succeed, as Scheherazade the storyteller had done in her nightly visits to whet the king's appetite for more the next night. Scheherazade had kept her head; Dorothy was determined to do the same.

She briefly summarised the latest Soviet threat, as she had been asked to do, but adding little that was new to what had already been reported in recent communications from Berlin and Moscow. She paused to look at the bored faces turned towards her. With impeccable timing worthy of an accomplished actor, she brushed aside the first intervention and drew attention to a new fact that had come into her hands as a result of the acquisition of collateral information. She paused again, looking up at those around the table, their pens poised above their notebooks. Dorothy relished this opportunity to mock the insufferable egos of her colleagues.

"Please continue, Mrs Maddox," said Menzies.

"Only if you think it worthwhile, C."

"Yes, of course you should continue," he replied dryly.

"Thank you, C." A look of satisfaction fleetingly crossed her face.

"A young British army officer, Major Richard Fortescue, a gifted linguist previously on secondment to the British prosecution team at Nuremburg, recently had a liaison with a young German woman whom he met in Munich at the end of last October."

"What on earth is the significance of that?" interrupted a short balding man. "We have more important matters to deal with than mere details of a young major's dalliance with a German national. She was probably a prostitute."

Dorothy gave Oliver Smyth an icy glare.

"May I continue? I suggest you withhold your comments, such as they may be, until I have finished."

"Touché," murmured Menzies.

"It would appear that the young woman's mother, Helga Eilers, was a trusted employee of Joseph Goebbels and in the latter phase of the war was part of his inner circle – to such an extent that it seems she became close to many of those around Hitler in the war's final months. I have reason to believe she was in the *Führerbunker* almost until the end – possibly up to twenty-four hours before he committed suicide. Her current whereabouts are unknown at this stage, though it is likely she may still be in hiding in Berlin, since according to Major Fortescue her daughter may recently have met her there. It would also appear that a few months before the end of the war, those close to Himmler deposited some secret files in a flat in Munich, rented by a young woman and shared by both Frau Eilers's daughter and her son. It is possible these files contained sensitive information for safe keeping in the event the war was lost. Amongst them was a black notebook, said to be in code, for Himmler's personal attention. The files were removed – by whom we do not know – and the young woman and Mrs Eilers's son were murdered – possibly by Nazi sympathisers. But the black book, hidden separately in the flat, is missing."

"This is all most intriguing, Mrs Maddox, but I don't see any connection to the Soviets and their activities in Berlin directed towards us and the Americans."

Her contempt seething, Dorothy replied with even greater cut.

"The black book was taken by Helga Eilers's daughter, Karin. We believe it is now in the possession of Major Fortescue."

"Then why doesn't his commanding officer order him to hand it over?"

"Major Fortescue has so far refused to reveal its whereabouts."

Another official at the table, Leonard Arkwright, pushed his notebook to one side and spoke, his words dripping with condescension.

"Mrs Maddox, thank you for this fascinating historical footnote but – though I am trying as hard as I can – I do not see any connection with the Russians, who as Mr Smyth has reminded us, are our preoccupation at the present time. Should we not move on, Chairman?"

Dorothy replied before Menzies could answer.

"Fräulein Eilers is currently in a Soviet jail in East Berlin awaiting trial for the attempted murder of a Russian officer who tried to rape her during her detention. In resisting his advances, she grabbed his sidearm from its holster and shot him. He survived. The key point is that the Soviets have Major Fortescue's army notebook, which regrettably Fräulein Eilers took by mistake from the room she was sharing with the Major the night before she was abducted by the Russians. In her haste, she mistook it for the notebook she had removed from the Munich flat. How the Soviets came to know about the Himmler notebook is unclear but, now aware of its existence, they want to get hold of it. From an examination of Fortescue's notebook, which possibly contains some sensitive information, they may have discovered an admission – he cannot remember if he wrote it down – that he shot an unknown German national in Seeshaupt, near Munich, last November. He claims he was acting in self-defence. I have been to see Fräulein Eilers several times thanks to the co-operation of Colonel Sokolov in Soviet military intelligence, whose acquaintance I made in Yalta. She refuses to say anything about what happened. As for her present position, the only thing that is likely to save her is Russian possession of the coded notebook and the seizure of Helga Eilers, whom I imagine they wish to question – as our people do – about Hitler's final hours. That is the Soviet connection."

"I am sorry, Mrs Maddox," said Arkwright, "but this is all rather thin and circumstantial. Be that as it may, are you suggesting that we find this notebook, the contents of which we don't know, and give it to the Russians? That's nonsense. If it contains information of value to us, we should keep it ourselves. The fate of the girl is of no concern to us. To do what you appear to be suggesting would turn us into a mere courier – with nothing substantial for us in return."

"C, I'm sorry but I don't see where this discussion is taking us. We should be talking about other matters," added Smyth.

"Mrs Maddox, I agree with my colleagues," said Menzies. "We should move on. What recommendation do you wish to make?"

"I have two. I recommend that we step up our search for Helga Eilers. If we find her, we and the Americans should surely question her, not the Russians. With regard to the notebook, it is highly desirable for us to gain possession of it as quickly as possible, so we can break the code and find out what information it contains. My second recommendation is therefore that, to force Major Fortescue to reveal the whereabouts of the notebook, he should be arrested and court-martialled."

"On what judicial grounds could such a step be taken?" Smyth asked.

"On the grounds of his admission that he killed a German national at Seeshaupt using his army-issued weapon unlawfully," replied Dorothy.

"But you have told us he says he shot the man in self-defence. Is his assertion not sufficient?" asked Clive Taylor, a younger man who so far had made no intervention.

"The German police in Munich have placed the Major and Fräulein Eilers in the village on that day. They were out walking when the shooting is alleged to have occurred. Moreover, the Major told me afterwards that he had shot a man who apparently threatened him and Fräulein Eilers. Immediately after the shooting, they left Seeshaupt for Munich. We need – for the sake of rebuilding the local police force – to put the evidence to the test in a court-martial."

"And, to clarify," said Menzies, "the intelligence rationale for such a step is … ?"

"To start putting Major Fortescue under an obligation to release the book to us rather than keep it concealed under the misplaced impression he can use it to barter the release of his girlfriend. But he is proving more stubborn than I thought."

"Is he likely to succumb to this increased pressure – the prospect of court-martial?" asked Taylor.

"We can only try," replied Dorothy.

"And what about his German girlfriend?" asked Smyth.

"I will continue to use my connection with Colonel Sokolov to see whether she can be treated leniently – in return for giving us more precise information about her mother's location in Berlin and who may be sheltering her. The sooner we find and arrest Helga Eilers the sooner we – rather than the Russians – will have possible further information about the last days in the bunker and the others who were there but who are still unaccounted for. We must play our part in quashing any speculation that Hitler has survived. The notebook and Helga Eilers are our business, not the Russians'."

"Would they let Miss Eilers go if she were more helpful?" asked Taylor.

"I doubt it," replied Dorothy. "More likely she will be sent to a camp in Russia for the purpose of sexual exploitation."

"And Fortescue's own notebook? What about that, and its implications for him?" Taylor asked.

"He is an unfortunate casualty of the war," said Dorothy. "If he is found guilty at his court-martial, his career will be finished."

"And what exactly should he be charged with?" asked Menzies.

"With the alleged murder of a German national, illegal use of his sidearm and withholding information of relevance to the security of this country," she answered. "Once he has been dealt with, and hopefully has surrendered the book to us, he will no longer be a threat to our operations in Berlin. We can then forget about him."

Smyth interjected. "I still don't see any connection between what Mrs Maddox has told us and current Soviet espionage activities in Berlin. But then perhaps I am missing a vital link in this rather odd story which I find somewhat lacking in elaboration."

Menzies asked for the views of others. No one added their voice.

"Please proceed to do as you have recommended, Mrs Maddox. Send a message to Nolan this evening."

"Yes, C," Dorothy replied.

"Like Mr Smyth, I still don't understand the significance of what we have agreed to do – what this story is all about. And I certainly don't see any Soviet connection. Perhaps I too have missed something."

"The discussion is over, Taylor," said Menzies firmly. "There is nothing more to be said on the matter. Now, I propose we break for five minutes before proceeding with our remaining business."

As they rose from the table, Philby entered the room, apologising for his late arrival.

"No need to apologise," said Menzies. "We've taken a decision – nothing relevant to your section's work."

As Menzies closed his folder, he saw inserted amongst his papers a reminder that the following evening he and Dorothy Maddox were to dine alone at his residence across the road in Queen Anne's Gate. This would be when he would hear more details of her important activity in East Berlin, about which he continued to have serious misgivings. One thing that could be said about her for sure was that she was a formidable woman to whom it was difficult to say no – even him.

Within three hours of the meeting Nolan received a telegram from headquarters instructing him to send a formal request to the Commandant seeking the immediate arrest and detention of Major Fortescue. He noticed that the message had been copied to Susannah Thomas's father, General Thomas.

It was past midnight before Dorothy went to bed. After reading more of Tolstoy's *War and Peace* she put the light out but found it difficult to sleep. It had been a long day and the Broadway meeting had not been as easy as she had anticipated. She knew her case for action had appeared weak – the connection between Fortescue and his girlfriend and the Russians may well have seemed opaque to those not in possession of all the details. Yet she had decided beforehand that was all she could say in the circumstances. Yes, there were several facts she had deliberately not disclosed to the meeting. But that was because she was unsure of the discretion, and perhaps even the loyalty, of some of those around the table.

Of course she felt guilt for the action that would now be taken against the young major and for disregarding his girlfriend, condemned to endure a Soviet prison to which she herself had delivered her. But post-war espionage was a deadly hard-fought game in which the stakes were pitilessly high. By stupidly becoming infatuated with a young attractive German woman instead of marrying his fiancée, Fortescue had unwittingly become a pawn in the supreme game of risk she was playing, his girlfriend likewise. If he suffered and Karin Eilers was found guilty of attempted murder, their plight would be a small price to pay for the bigger prize she was seeking. After all, she had learned at SOE that military personnel sometimes had to make critical life and death decisions, often where the answer was not morally clear. In an SOE operation that she had planned, she had at the last moment been denied an opportunity to demonstrate her skill, bravery and loyalty to her country. She was determined not to be denied this time. The consequences of what she was planning had to be borne whatever the cost, a point she would make to C the next day.

* * * * *

While Dorothy slept, eventually, in her Pimlico flat, her bed heavy with blankets against the intense cold, Helga Eilers shivered in a small dismal room in Spandau she had rented cheaply for a few weeks. It was not far from the guest house Helmut told her about, where she had stayed only briefly. She would have stayed longer but the proprietor had warned his boarders that the British military were increasing document checks on all hotel guests in order to catch criminals, black-market operators and those from the lower rungs of the Nazi regime not yet screened for possible culpability. She read the newspapers daily. Three days into her stay she noted in *Der Tagesspiegel* a list of those being sought and the offer of a reward for information about their whereabouts. For the first time, her name was on the list. She put the newspaper down, her hands momentarily trembling. She felt desperately alone and vulnerable. All the promises of assistance she had been given had come to nothing. She looked at the grainy picture of her printed in the article, taken, she recalled, from a group photograph at the Berghof, and compared it with the disguised image in her forged identity document, bearing the name Ingrid Becker and prepared for her use while she was living in the cellar. She then turned to look at herself in the mirror. The glamorous Helga she had once been – the Helga who had been to bed with many in Hitler's circle, who had danced with the men who had surrounded Eva Braun – had become an aged, dowdy woman who would not now turn any man's head. But while the Helga of the past had gone, at least her grey hair, lined face, stooped frame and persistent cough from months in the cellar would serve her well in her disguise.

There had been times in the past days when she had considered surrendering to the British. Better them any day than those barbarian Russians who raped any woman they could get their hands on, regardless of her age. But she could never bring herself to do so. The thought of examination and the prospect of being tried for her activities, including for her involvement – though more incidental than significant – in procedures connected to the shipment of some remaining Jewish families from Grunewald station to the East, underlined her lack of any moral principles. But then she had always been weak, a good-time girl turned by pleasure without compassion or scruple. She had lost her husband long ago, murdered by SS thugs of the sort whose company she had come to enjoy. She had long neglected her son, Gerhard, who had suffered badly in the army, not just from the privations of the Russian Front but from the exhausting effort of hiding his homosexuality. Ultimately, he had been "executed" for not fighting for the regime to the end, but she suspected it was more likely because his shameful secret had been revealed.

As for her daughter, she had always been independent – a striking, well-educated, free-thinking young woman who attracted men as she herself had once done, but in Karin's case she was able to do it without flaunting her body. The last she knew of her was that she was in Russian hands. She could only imagine what they were doing to her. Yet these grim reflections, her gnawing sense of guilt, did not detract from her stubborn instinct for survival. She took out her picture of Hitler, running her fingers across the image of the man she had adored for so long, recalling the time she had met him, shaken his hand. He had remained alive as long as he could in the hope that the tide might turn. She too still hoped, in her tenaciously self-preserving way, that come the spring, when the miserable Berlin winter would be behind her, she would finally be able to leave the city and with the money she had left perhaps open a small shop in the western part of Germany, as far away as possible. She just had to get through the next few weeks, playing the part of a nondescript old woman no one could conceivably identify as the dazzling confidante of Magda Goebbels. To complete the part, she would buy herself a walking stick.

* * * * *

The prison regime for Karin became ever harsher. She had not seen Mrs Maddox for over two weeks, so her supply of small items she could barter in return for being left alone had diminished to a few nondescript items that carried little value. Her prison garb provided barely any warmth at night; each day, she worked in the prison laundry, ironing an endless supply of coarse military uniforms. In what little time she had to herself, she tried to read more of the book Richard Fortescue had given her. As she read, she not only imagined the warmth of Italy but also remembered the time she and he had spent together, in Munich but more particularly at Seeshaupt, when they had sat beside the fire while he had questioned her about her past and then danced to Beethoven before making love. But these memories did not last long, drowned out by the incessant Soviet music blaring over the tannoy or the forced recitation of passages from the Communist manifesto. She invented a crude code and listed on a scrap of paper the names of the prison guards she would come to haunt after her likely execution, driving them to the madness they were inflicting on her. Night after night, wrapped in her filthy blanket, she prayed she would be left alone. But one night her prayers went unanswered.

Two young Soviet soldiers – perhaps non-commissioned officers, judging by their epaulettes – inebriated with vodka, came to the cell block looking for sexual gratification. They came to the cell Karin shared with another, older woman and unlocked the door.

"Hey, Ivan, here's the bitch who shot Kovalev. She's about to be tried, so not much time to fuck her. Who's going to be first?"

"You go first, Sergei. But don't let her get hold of your gun. She might shoot you."

The two soldiers raped her savagely before doing the same to her companion and then moving on to the next cell. Karin wept, from physical pain and from the shame of her violation. Was there no end to her nightmare? Suddenly there was a commotion. She thought more soldiers were coming to satiate their appetite. Shots rang out followed by screams of agony. She could not imagine what new horrors were about to visit her. There were more running feet. Then the block fell quiet, plunged into darkness. A few minutes later the key in the lock turned. A shadow bent over her. Karin froze in fear. But the shadow put a gentle hand on her shoulder.

"It's me, Colonel Sokolov. I deeply regret what they did to you. It should not have happened. They were second-echelon soldiers. There are still some like them left in Berlin – either previously prisoners of the German army or petty criminals pressed into service."

"They were animals. Is that what the Soviet Union stands for? Put me before your so-called court, try me, find me guilty and execute me. I no longer wish to live in this cage," said Karin between her sobs.

"Fräulein, you will be tried, have no fear of that. Until then, I am placing you in solitary confinement where I can keep a closer eye on your safety. Come with me."

He helped her scoop up her few possessions and she followed him down the hall, stumbling from the pain in her thighs. At the entrance, in the gloom, she noticed two soldiers on the floor, being tended to. Sokolov turned to her.

"They won't do that again. I shot their balls off."

Several minutes later she entered another small cell. As she sat down on the truckle bed, Sokolov wrapped a blanket around her shoulders, whispering in her ear, "Mrs Maddox is coming to see you soon. In the morning, I will see that you have some fresh clothes. I don't want to suffer one of her reprimands for failing to take care of an important prisoner." He turned away, locking the cell door behind him. Karin fingered the length of cord secreted around her waist. She had once read that there was no salvation without sacrifice. Though she was a survivor by nature, the prospects facing her were so bleak that perhaps the time had come to hang herself.

* * * * *

On Tuesday 28 January, Richard Fortescue was arrested by the military police and placed in a secure room at the back of Lancaster House. It had a comfortable bed, a table and some reading material to supplement the few books he had been permitted to bring with him, including his thick volume of all of Shakespeare's plays and sonnets. The spine was torn, with the consequence that the entire book was tied together with string to stop it falling apart. Following his arrest, his lodging and personal possessions had been searched, but the black book everyone was looking for had not been found. He knew they would not find it because he had it with him. He had cut out a rectangle in the last hundred pages of the Shakespeare tome into which he had slotted the notebook. How careless the RMPs had been. Nothing like that would have happened at Nuremburg – with one exception. Göring had managed to secrete a phial of poison, which he took shortly before his scheduled hanging. The Americans had been negligent – not just in their search of his cell but in their regular observation of the prisoner. Fortescue was asked whether there was anything he required. He requested a gramophone player and his few recordings of Bach, which he had bought in Berlin.

The following morning, he received a message from his guard that during the afternoon he would have a visit from Mrs Maddox. Before then he faced another interrogation by Nolan, but this time in the presence of a military lawyer, Major Petworth, assigned to represent him. It was during his hour with Nolan that Fortescue began to realise Dorothy Maddox might have betrayed his confidence. That would explain how his accusers were so well-briefed. If that were the case, there had been a material and damaging change in his position. For once, his self-confidence was shaken. Now he had his back to the proverbial wall. What should he do next?

* * * * *

The evening before Dorothy Maddox's return to Berlin, Stewart Menzies received her at his residence. He had seen a number of women from the SOE absorbed into MI6 since the end of the war. They were a welcome addition, since they brought with them some *joie de vivre*, a sense of daring and a talent for the unexpected. But he was less interested in the role they might play. The male incumbents within his organisation, no doubt threatened by the women's skills, bravery and humour, had not taken well to their arrival, as Dorothy herself had found out. Menzies had long admired her, for her quiet demeanour, her intelligence, her grace and her stubbornness. She had borne the loss of her husband with commendable fortitude, in his view. The emptiness it had undoubtedly left had been filled with a fierce commitment to her work, as reports he had perused indicated. But there was another aspect to Dorothy. She had a physical magnetism that men found attractive. Though often appearing serious and locked in concentration, she could release a captivating smile. He could well believe the stories that this tall, slim woman, who dressed well in fashionable figure-hugging clothes and who wore heels with sublime confidence, was the subject of bets within the office as to who could bed her first.

The two ate supper on a card table set before the fire. As they chatted about the latest London social gossip, the windows rattled in the chilling wind. Over coffee, the conversation turned to Berlin.

"You were tough on Fortescue at the meeting. You are a driven woman, Dorothy, as I was warned before you joined us. But you were hard in recommending his arrest. He did well in Nuremburg and there are people in London keen to recruit him. His arrest will ruin his reputation, unless he is acquitted. You take no prisoners, as they say."

"No, I do not," she replied. "We have bigger fish to fry. Minnows must not be allowed to get in the way."

"So I see," said Menzies, smiling.

"That's the way it has to be, C, as I hope you will agree."

"How is your project progressing? Are you making progress? Is he taking the bait?"

"He is softening. But more needs to be done. It will take a little while yet. I ask you not to say a word to anyone else at Broadway. There are some I would personally not trust."

"Is that because of their education?" he asked.

"No. Where they went to school, or their university, does not bother me. It's their loyalty to the cause that concerns me. I want to finish this as we agreed – with no one else knowing."

"I understand, Dorothy. You have my word. I won't even tell Philby."

"Good. He concerns me more than the others."

"But if what you intend to do goes wrong, we won't save you. The service will deny all knowledge and you will be finished, disowned, washed up. You must understand that."

"I do," she replied.

With that, supper ended and Dorothy left Queen Anne's Gate.

CHAPTER ELEVEN

The Reckoning

Helga Eilers – or Ingrid Becker, as she kept having to remind herself – walked slowly back to her room in Spandau, pulling behind her a small wooden handcart in which was a meagre bag of coal, some pieces of firewood and a few items of food she had bought from a streetside seller. The war had been over almost two years but the privations in the city seemed – at least to her – to have eased little. Her boots, much in need of fresh soles, slipped on the ice lodged in the gaps left by cobblestones pulled up by the remnants of the Hitler Youth to throw at the advancing Russian army as it fanned out across the city in May 1945. She had wound black material around her hands to protect an expensive pair of black leather gloves given to her by one of her SS admirers. The baker had reminded her it was the 28th of February but there was still no sign of spring. She paused for breath. If only she could leave Berlin, full of the ghosts of the past, full of memories. It was becoming painful to remember. But judging by the newspapers and gossip on street corners, it was difficult for Berliners to make the journey to the West. The city was encircled by Soviet forces and a new hostile East German regime was emerging, adding to the pressure on the western part of the city. Much as she would like to escape, she was not confident enough to try her luck at the Russian side of the Dreilinden checkpoint. For the present, without help to access an escape route, she was stuck. She cursed.

Sensing somebody coming up behind her, she resumed her pace, the recalcitrant cart with its squeaking wheel at her heels. She slipped again as she turned the corner but a strong hand grasped her by the arm.

"Careful, Frau Becker," said a voice. "I caught you just in time."

She looked up. She had seen the grizzled face before – a near neighbour – but she could not remember his name.

"Thank you."

"Where's your stick? You usually have it with you."

"I thought I could manage without it today. How wrong I was."

"Not like the good old days," said the man, now walking alongside her, supporting her elbow. She inwardly resented him doing so.

"It was a fine city then," he continued. "Things got done. Everyone knew their place. It all went wrong with those damn enemy air raids – the Americans and the British. Now they are here, they behave as though they own the lot. And then there are those damn Russians in the East, killing and raping if the rumours are true. If only the generals hadn't let him down. Were you in Berlin then?"

"Yes," she replied, wishing her unwanted companion would go away.

"Once it was such a fine city," he said again. "And those parades ... Now ruin. Nothing left. Where will it end?"

She nearly uttered words of commiseration, recalling the Führer's rants against the army, which she had heard while in the bunker. But her cracked lips remained sealed.

"Are you all right now? Do you want help to carry these things upstairs?"

"No thank you. I can manage."

With that they parted. She still could not remember his name.

She closed the door behind her and sat down. Hidden in Spandau, she thought it would be easy to bury her past, to begin anew. But the dreary tedium of daily life, marked by few possessions, the biting cold and her dependence on the generosity of neighbours who had taken pity on an ageing war widow, was steadily wearing away her remaining self-esteem and determination to survive like the drip of water on limestone. She felt increasingly lonely. Each night she nursed herself to sleep with the ever-diminishing memories of the past. She sometimes woke in the small hours and thought that perhaps her hardship – and Hitler's defeat – had all been a bad dream. But as dawn broke, the bleakness of the landscape beyond the window, the intense cold and the lack of fresh clothes to wear were a painful reminder that it was only too real. Over and over again, she asked herself why the help to escape she had been promised had failed to materialise. Why had she been left behind? She had been attractive, loyal to the cause until the end and there had been no shortage of men in uniform – some very handsome – who had sought their way into her bed. Surely that should have counted? Perhaps very few had survived the final Russian onslaught.

The following afternoon, again seeking comfort from the past, she removed from its cloth wrapping a small photograph album, kept in her case together with her money, the pictures of Hitler and Goebbels, her Party membership card and her diamond swastika pendant and ring. She slowly thumbed through the pages, each image telling the story of her rising career in the Propaganda Ministry. There was one photo she liked especially – almost the best – taken, she thought, in the summer of 1940. Hitler was standing in front of his desk in the Reich Chancellery about to shake hands with a tall slender aristocratic-looking woman with her back to the camera, dark wavy hair tumbling to her shoulders and wearing a narrow-brimmed hat set to one side of her head, a floral skirt, a short close-fitting jacket and high heels. Behind a smiling Hitler stood Helga, in a tight-waisted dress and beaming into the lens, relishing her proximity to the Führer. She could not remember the name of Hitler's visitor – she had stupidly failed to record the date and her name on the back of the photo – but she recalled she had been striking and poised, an example she had subsequently tried to emulate. That evening Helga had been part of a celebration following further positive news from France. What a contrast. Now she was penniless and in hiding, pretending to be an aged woman, though in reality that is exactly what she had become.

Just over a week later, on Tuesday 11 March, as the weather began to show improvement, Helga decided to get out of her suffocating room and take a bus ride to the city centre. She dusted her boots, brushed her coat, adjusted her hat rather in the style of the woman in the picture, and applied a modicum of make-up. She set out, walking stick in hand, constantly reminding herself to hobble in case her nosy neighbour saw her. Since the end of the war, she had stayed away from the city centre, going only rarely, because visits there brought back too many painful memories and she was terrified of being recognised. At the time of her escape from the bunker in May 1945 she had been shocked at the devastation around her as the Russians continued to pound the city with heavy artillery.

Now, almost two years later, it seemed to her there had been little change. Though there was more business activity there were still ruined buildings, still piles of rubble, albeit now diminished in size, and still traces of the pungent smell of death. She observed there were more people about, more traffic and some of the shops damaged during the war had reopened. Yet she still perceived hunched haunted figures who looked down as they navigated the streets, like ghosts in a city of the dead, a city with its once proud spirit still entombed in a landscape of destruction and ugliness. After walking along the Kurfürstendamm, peering into shop windows, she decided to find somewhere to have a coffee before returning to her shoebox of a room. She knew from her occasional outings in Spandau that real coffee was hard to get and expensive when it was available. More often than not the promised high-quality coffee turned out to be hot brown water. But the sun had momentarily broken through the clouds and though the café she had just passed looked expensive she could not resist retracing her steps.

There were few inside, which put her at her ease. Those who were there were elderly, both men and women, gossiping as Berliners do, or reading newspapers. As it was warm inside, she shed her coat and placed it over her shoulders as she used to do in the old days. Just as she was ordering the cheapest coffee available, three uniformed British soldiers entered and sat near the window. Judging by their red caps they were military police. Their presence caused her a momentary frisson of fear. Resisting the temptation to put on her coat and leave – she imagined the scene it might cause, being pursued by the waitress asking why she was not going to drink what she had ordered – she decided to stay, confident in her disguise of a dowdy grey-haired elderly woman. Besides, the war had ended two years before and no one had ever challenged her. As she sipped her coffee and savoured each mouthful of a small pastry, she glanced at a copy of *Der Tagesspiegel*, reading reports of the worsening relationship between the Soviet Union and the Western Allies and how, unless it were soon resolved, it would have an impact on the already tense situation in Berlin. She sat for almost an hour. Realising that it would soon be dark, she prepared, reluctantly, to leave. As she signalled to the waitress for the bill, a man got up from a table across the room and walked towards her. He pulled back a chair and sat opposite her.

"I believe we've met once before," he said softly, as if not wanting to be overheard by the approaching waitress.

After paying her bill, she turned to him.

"I don't think we have. You must be mistaken."

"I'm not mistaken," he replied, looking at her intently. "I have a good memory for faces. That was important in my job."

"That's of no concern to me." She could smell his alcoholic breath. His manner was menacing.

"You are Frau Helga Eilers, are you not?"

"No, I am Frau Ingrid Becker. Now, will you please make way? I wish to leave." She too spoke quietly, trying to keep the panic from her voice.

"You are not Ingrid Becker. You are Helga Eilers. You were a secretary in Goebbels's office. Always stuck-up but you did well for yourself and rose up the ladder."

She looked at him, trying to place his face. Her heart was beating quickly and the palms of her hands were sweaty. He moved to sit beside her.

"Let me jog your memory. I am Ernst Frank. I used to be an auxiliary driver at Gestapo headquarters. I drove you once to the Chancellery. You had a good figure then and I recall you flashed nice legs as you got out of the car. And I saw you again at the Berghof. I was driving the car behind yours. Now you look a bit of a mess – not the elegant woman you once were. So, own up, you're Helga Eilers, aren't you?" He nudged her with his shoulder.

"Yes," she whispered in reply. She felt faint.

"Like you, I'm wanted for questioning," he said. "But I'm small fry. I'm sure you're higher up the pecking order. You must know a lot of secrets from those days."

One of the British soldiers had got up from the table, looking around as if searching for something. He headed towards them. As he passed, Frank put his arm around Helga.

"Give her a kiss, mate," the soldier urged, leering. "She needs cheering up."

Frank smiled at him.

"I think we should leave now," said Helga. "I've got a bus to catch."

"So have I – to your place, Frau Eilers. I need somewhere to stay for a day or so, while I find my feet. Like you, I've had a hard time."

"I have no room," Helga said as they left the café.

"No matter, I'll sleep on the floor. Just as long as it's warm. Or I can share your bed. After all, you were known amongst us lowly drivers as an SS bed-warmer. It seems you were less keen on the Gestapo. They didn't have those flashy SS uniforms you appeared to like."

"And if I can't help you?" she asked, tiring of his presence. She tried to think what she could do to get rid of him. Perhaps she could promise him something and then lose him in the crowd. Or walk up a side street and knee him in the groin. He read her thoughts.

"Don't even think about giving me the slip. If you did, I

would find you. I'm good at following people. You and I have got to stick together. Besides, if you don't help a fellow Nazi on the run, I'll turn you in and earn some credit. These days good information can be worth a lot of money."

Helga looked at him. She was conscious that her hands were shaking. How had she been so stupid as to leave her room at the least hint of spring, to put her true identity at risk of being discovered for the sake of a coffee? Now she was cornered by one of those unpleasant thugs loyal to Himmler.

"Well, where are we going?" Frank asked.

"To Spandau," she replied.

They walked to the bus stop, his arm in hers, his grip on her hand tight.

It took over an hour to return to Spandau. As they walked along her street, the familiar neighbour who had recently come to her rescue passed them and doffed his hat.

"Have a nice evening, Frau Becker. Good to see you've got someone to keep you company today."

She smiled weakly at him.

Later, Helga and Frank ate what little food she had left, sitting in front of a meagre fire. They spoke little for the rest of the evening. After drinking a couple of stiff vodkas from a bottle she had long kept aside, he fell asleep in the chair. She was tempted to strike him with the poker in her rage at his unwanted intrusion into her life. But he might resist and the neighbours might hear their struggle. And if she killed him outright, how would she dispose of his body? Or she could consume the phial of poison she kept and end her life, leaving him with the consequences. Realising there was little she could do until the morning she put a blanket over him, drank the remnants of the vodka and went to bed. In the small hours, after the fire had died, he came into her bed, putting his arm around her tightly. She thought he would try to force himself on her but he did not. Soon, she drifted off into a fitful sleep.

When she woke, Frank was gone. On the mantelpiece, she found a note thanking her for her hospitality and generosity and wishing her well in eluding justice and finding a new life. She went to her case. All her precious personal belongings were still there but to her horror the roll of money, held together by a frayed rubber band and which she had saved so carefully, had gone. Apart from a few marks in her purse, she had nothing left, not enough to pay her next rent. She sat down and buried her face in her hands. The bastard had left her destitute. She sat beside the lifeless fire and, cradling a mug of hot water, tried to think what she should do – commit suicide, appeal to her neighbours for charity, try to get a job, or earn some money shifting rubble as many other women did.

Later that morning, she decided. It was time to leave Spandau, to do something different. She unpacked her green silk dress, all that was left of her past life – a dress she had last worn in the company of Eva Braun in the closing months of the war. After applying some lipstick and rouge and brushing her hair, she put on some patent heeled shoes that she had bought in a street market, followed by her coat, hat and gloves. Carrying only her small brown leather case, she left her shabby room and shut the front door, posting the keys through the letterbox.

"Good morning, Frau Becker," said her neighbour. "You look smart today. I hope you are going somewhere special."

She smiled. "Perhaps," she answered.

She walked into the main part of town. As she crossed the bridge, and while she thought no one was looking, she tossed the case into the water. She watched as it floated downstream. She wiped a tear from her face and walked on.

A few minutes later she entered a building.

"Can I help you?"

"Yes, please," she replied. "I am Frau Helga Eilers and I have come to give myself up for questioning."

The police officer looked at her. "Are you sure?"

"Yes," she replied. "I'm sure."

Within two hours Helga was in British military custody, formally arrested, photographed, and searched. She sat in a cell, a warm, simple meal on a tin plate resting on her knees. The only item left from her precious possessions was the small phial of poison she had secreted in her vagina.

* * * * *

Later that evening, Dorothy Maddox asked the sentry who had been ordered to check on the prisoner from time to time to stand aside. She quietly slid back the aperture in the cell door. Here was precious fruit that had fallen into her hands. She would shortly question Richard Fortescue for the second time since her return from London, trying again to persuade him to reveal the whereabouts of the black book.

* * * * *

No report appeared in the Berlin newspapers about Helga Eilers's surrender to the authorities. This diminished interest in the fate of less important people in the Nazi Party machine was not surprising. With the end of war receding in memory and with other more pressing matters of concern, the British had effectively passed responsibility for the de-Nazification process to the Berlin police. However, inevitably, news of her arrest quickly reached the Soviet authorities through their eyes and ears in the western sectors, prompting an official request through the Allied Kommandatura for access. As part of their investigation of Hitler's final days and the whereabouts of some senior figures not yet apprehended, they were keen to question her about her period in the *Führerbunker* prior to Hitler's death and the means of her escape. There was some surprise when the request was made so quickly and that it should concern such an unimportant figure. But it was of no surprise to Dorothy Maddox and Charles Nolan. The Russians received a polite reply that their request would be considered in due course. For their part, the Americans showed only moderate interest in Helga Eilers and, though offered the opportunity to observe her interrogation, they declined.

Colonel Sokolov put the Soviet request for access to Helga Eilers at the top of what he called his Maddox agenda, to discuss when she next came to Karlshorst. While he was encouraged that his prisoner's mother was now in British custody, thereby possibly providing the basis for an eventual exchange, the nub of the problem remained unresolved: the fate of the black book, which it was increasingly urgent should come into his hands. Like others, he wanted to see its contents, about which there were so many rumours. All he knew from Dorothy Maddox was that the book was in the hands of a British major. When they next met, he would propose the release of Karin Eilers in return for the book and her mother Helga. While the latter had little intrinsic value, nonetheless she was a good cover for his real objective. Despite remarks by senior officers that he was giving a German woman special treatment, over the past weeks he had managed to delay the start of Karin Eilers's trial, arguing that Kovalev needed to be fully fit to deliver his testimony. He had even gone to the trouble of getting him extra medical attention in Moscow to push back the date even further. Once Kovalev returned to active duty in Berlin, Sokolov knew he would be able to delay no longer.

During this time, Karin had remained in solitary confinement. She said very little each day during her brief exercise period and when alone she read, mostly Soviet literature Colonel Sokolov had given her. After a while she began to learn Russian with the help of a warder. But the constant observation, the dampness of her cell and the pervasive fear of further sexual assault did little to raise her spirits. For her, the trial would be the beginning of the end. She was under no illusion about the outcome: death or many years' hard labour. There was no pity for Germans. At last, she received written notification that her trial for attempted murder of a Soviet officer would begin on Tuesday 25 March 1947. Major Alexei Morozov would defend her.

* * * * *

Richard Fortescue spent considerable time during his period of arrest reflecting on his predicament, reading and answering several emotional letters from Susannah, and trying to decipher the encrypted black book. He replied to each of Susannah's letters, in which she repeatedly proclaimed her loyalty and love however long it might take to clear his name of the unjustified charge brought against him, thanking her for her support and affection but urging her to forget him. Whatever the outcome of the process he faced, he had proved unworthy of a woman from such a prestigious military family. She deserved a life of happiness and fulfilment, pride and respect, not one overshadowed by the likely lasting stain to his reputation. Moreover, he would no longer be able to pursue his army career, which would only add to her disappointment and that of her family. Though he repeated this message in each reply, it seemed to make little difference. Susannah's letters became even more anguished and painful to read. Receipt of each only served to remind him of Karin, of the time they had spent together in Seeshaupt – dancing together, in bed together. If he had not insisted on buying her a coffee in that seedy bar and persuading her to accompany him to the opera in Munich, she would not now be in a Soviet prison and he would be back in London. He had to make amends.

Every evening, alone in his locked room, he scrutinised over and over again each page of the notebook still hidden in the Shakespeare volume. To inspire his analysis – and to annoy his guard – he played his Bach records continuously. He admired the composer's spiritual craft, his precise musical notation and mental discipline. His favourite was the *Violin Concerto in D Minor*.

Though not a code-breaker, only a crossword devotee, he was certain his first impression had been right – that at least part of the neatly written book comprised a list of names, concealed in some kind of random code. Late one evening, after many hours looking for similarities and weaknesses, he suddenly realised it was possible that not all of the names were German – in a few cases the code-maker appeared to have had difficulty transcribing the words into the cipher he was using, perhaps because they were written in a foreign alphabet with which he was less familiar. The following night Fortescue tried different combinations of letters, using small squares of paper on each of which he had written a character. It was like putting together a fiendishly difficult jigsaw. He tried hard to remember some of the code books he had casually looked at while in Nuremburg, including one, known as a *Schlüsselanleitung zum*

Rufzeichenschlüssel – a key instruction to call-sign key – that had caused great excitement at Bletchley Park in November 1944. Unable to sleep, he got up and looked at the black book yet again.

On the next evening, after he had been locked up for the night, he decided to focus on one entry that seemed to be weaker in its code than the others, perhaps because the writer had become fatigued and frustrated and therefore less careful in his transcription. He wrote down each letter of the coded word on fresh squares of paper, constantly rearranging them in different combinations. Suddenly, he stumbled on a run of five letters that made sense: s-o-k-o-l. He remembered once reading that "sokol" was the root of the Russian surname Sokolov, often said to mean a bird of prey. The five letters were accompanied by a prefix "V".

Despite further efforts, he could not break the code to unscramble any other names in the book. Nor was he the wiser as to whether the people listed were enemies of the state marked for possible liquidation or sympathetic to the Nazi regime and marked for a different purpose. If they were enemies, they might already have been executed in the final frenzy of the war, when all those who had failed to stop the Russian advance into Berlin were murdered. But if they were not enemies, there must have been another reason for drawing them to Himmler's attention. As the list appeared to be dated December 1944, the latter possibility seemed to Fortescue the more likely, with the reason being that they might provide assistance to the *Reichsführer* in one way or another. In the light of this thinking, he once again examined the names – numbering more than one hundred and, uncharacteristically, apparently not in alphabetical order as was usually the case with SS documentation – to see whether there were any other inconsistencies in the random code. He again focused on the idea of foreign names.

He suddenly remembered Count Folke Bernadotte, a Swedish diplomat and nobleman who had negotiated the release of tens of thousands of prisoners from German concentration camps, including hundreds of Danish Jews from the camp at Theresienstadt, and to whom Himmler had sent a surrender offer, which had been rejected. After further painstaking use of variations, he uncovered a misspelt version of the Count's name. Its inclusion appeared to confirm that the book was probably a list not of enemies for execution but of possible contacts to approach for one purpose or another if the Reich finally fell. If his supposition and decoding were correct, and if the Sokolov listed in the book was the same man that Dorothy Maddox had been meeting regularly in Karlshorst, it was possible her contact had had intelligence connections with the Nazis – perhaps through the *Abwehr*, the German military intelligence organisation, which had existed until 1945 and which he had been told MI6 had penetrated.

Did this suggest a connection between Berlin and Moscow which Himmler wished to pursue in the last desperate months of the war? And did MI6 know of the link? Had they turned Sokolov into a British agent? Was that the real reason why Dorothy Maddox went so often to Karlshorst – not to see Karin but, using her as cover, to receive information from Sokolov? Was she his handler? Was the hunt for the book an effort to suppress information of this treachery within Soviet military intelligence? Had it been a Russian agent, anxious to get hold of the book because Soviet intelligence was suspicious of Sokolov, whom he had shot in Seeshaupt? Or had it been someone else – perhaps from an ex-Nazi organisation keen to protect those named in the book and able to help spirit SS and Gestapo comrades out of Germany? Fortescue sensed he had happened upon highly sensitive information. If he had, he intended to use it to his advantage – in his own trial for alleged murder but also to secure Karin's freedom, provided she were still alive and safe in East Berlin. He would also use it in his next meeting with Dorothy.

His first meeting with her following her return from London, at which they were joined by Charles Nolan, had been short. She had still shown the same warmth of friendship as in their earlier conversations. But while sympathetic to his plight – her words not his – she had focused the discussion – allegedly off the record – on the whereabouts of the book. It would make his position easier, she said, if he told them without further ado where it was. She and her colleagues needed to get their hands on it. It was not his to keep and it could conceivably contain information that the Allies could follow up to ensure those guilty of war crimes were held accountable. Once again, much to her obvious irritation, he had declined to provide the information she and Nolan sought. In the light of his discovery, he would at their next meeting play a game with her.

Dorothy was once again accompanied by Charles Nolan. Sitting beside Fortescue was Major James Petworth, who had been appointed as his defence counsel. Nolan informed him that the court-martial would take place in Berlin on Monday 14 April, immediately after Easter. He was charged with the alleged killing of a German national, the unauthorised use of a British army weapon to commit the alleged act, and withholding information bearing on national security. There was a short discussion about the procedures to be followed and the evidence that would be presented by the prosecution – largely based on eyewitness statements obtained by the Munich police and his admission to Mrs Maddox that he had fired his gun, purportedly in self-defence. Major Petworth sought the necessary authorisations to enable him to talk alone to his client.

As the meeting drew to a close, Fortescue requested Dorothy to remain behind to discuss another matter that had come to his attention. He asked Petworth to go with Nolan to ensure that the conversation he and Mrs Maddox were about to have would not be recorded and listened in to. Nolan's face reddened.

"I don't do things like that," he remonstrated.

"Whether you do or you don't, I want to make sure that it does not happen on this occasion. I suggest that Major Petworth sits in your office, in case I need him later. He can watch what you do with your hands – and ears – while Mrs Maddox and I are together."

Nolan protested. Dorothy turned to him.

"Charles, please do as he asks."

Neither Fortescue nor Dorothy spoke after the door closed. The game of cat and mouse had begun. Who would break the silence first? It was Dorothy.

"I was at Karlshorst yesterday to fulfil my promise to see Miss Eilers. Her trial is finally set for later this month, though it is possible it may be further delayed. She's bearing up well in solitary confinement. Colonel Sokolov arranged that degree of comfort, if you can call it comfort, after two drunken soldiers got into the prison and raped her."

Fortescue's face flushed with anger.

"The likely verdict is guilty, I imagine."

"Perhaps," replied Dorothy. "I will do my best for her."

"As you once did for me?"

"I did what was necessary in a difficult situation."

"You're an attractive woman, Mrs Maddox. Just as you were in SOE – one of those beguiling good-looking women sent into Europe to set honeytraps to catch the enemy. Well, you certainly set one for me in Munich. You won my trust, helped me with Fräulein Eilers. I told you in great confidence what had happened at Seeshaupt. You provided me with a bullet in case my alibi was questioned. I thanked you. You gave me help and advice in Berlin. Then you disappear to London and while you're gone I'm charged on your evidence with murder. How's that for undying friendship? Was it not Publio who said to the Emperor in *La clemenza di Tito*, 'He who is always true often fails to see disloyalty in others'?"

"I had to do it. I can say no more."

"I sense, Mrs Maddox, that at present I'm a tiresome irritant in the way of some bigger plan at 54 Broadway. I'm the grit in the proverbial oyster, not the pearl."

"I cannot comment other than to say I have to do as instructed."

"How often did I hear similar words at Nuremburg? 'I was under orders.'"

Dorothy's patience snapped.

"Major Fortescue, it would help all of us if you stopped playing silly games and told us where you have hidden the notebook that Miss Eilers removed from the Munich flat. As

I've said before, it's not yours to keep. It belongs to the investigating authorities. If you hand it over, we'll pass it on to Detective Hessler. It will make things easier for you too."

"I bet you'll pass it on to Hessler, a two-bit copper from Munich. I'm sure you people want it for your own secret purposes," he snapped back.

"See sense, Major, please."

"I am, Mrs Maddox, I am."

"I'm doing my best for you, Richard. I really am."

"Are you? Knifing me in the back?"

Fortescue stood up to look out of the barred window. Now he would strike. Take her by surprise as he had sometimes done at Nuremburg, when the clever defendant thought his lies had convinced the interrogator.

"What would you say if I told you that Colonel Sokolov's name appears in the black book – a book that was prepared in secrecy and obviously in some haste for Himmler?"

Dorothy appeared stunned, momentarily lost for words.

"You seem surprised."

"I would need to see the book, as indeed would others. Richard, I ask you again. Please hand over the book. You are getting out of your depth."

Fortescue sat down and leaned across the table.

"I will hand it over, but only on my terms."

"And what are those?" Dorothy asked.

"First, that once you and your colleagues have seen the book, you confirm to me that Sokolov's name is in it – and you have to tell me the truth. Assuming it is, then I want you to use that fact to oblige him to release Karin as quickly as possible, unharmed, and to bring her into the British sector."

"And your other terms?" she asked.

"I want the charges against me dropped with full exoneration and, of course, authorisation to take Karin with me to England if she will come."

"When will you hand over the book?"

"When I'm released and she is with me."

"The Russians don't operate like that, as you well know. They will want to see the book first."

"Well, perhaps it's time to change the rules."

Dorothy said nothing. She looked at Fortescue.

"I must consult London. I cannot give you an answer now. Let us talk again tomorrow. The answer may well be no. You may just have to give us the book."

* * * * *

As Dorothy prepared to leave Lancaster House, she reflected on the unexpected development to her plan. Assuming Fortescue was telling the truth, and had not misconstrued what was written in the book, his assertion would seem to bear out a fragment of uncorroborated information she had recently read in London, from where MI6 had operated their own channels into the *Abwehr*. If Sokolov had indeed been in touch with German military intelligence earlier in the war – whether because of German sympathies or as a double agent to secure vital military deployment information – this added a new dimension to the man she was about to see once again, and to her pursuit of the truth about him. Her search for it had begun in Yalta. Perhaps she was now close to finding it. She concluded that she would recommend deferment of Fortescue's court-martial and seek authorisation for the immediate implementation of the project in East Berlin on which she had briefed C in London.

Meanwhile, it would be necessary to mount another search for the black book without Fortescue's knowledge. She seldom acted on anyone's terms but her own, and had no intention of acceding to Fortescue's. But he could not be threatened any further. To do so might result in his misguided affection for the Eilers woman causing her organisation considerable embarrassment, particularly if he began to disclose what he had already told her.

As she was putting on her coat, she received information that Helga Eilers had acknowledged, during questioning, her involvement in the disclosure to the Gestapo of some of the participants in the July 1944 plot against Hitler, leading to their arrest and execution.

CHAPTER TWELVE

Loyal or False?

Dorothy Maddox sat in the telegrams room waiting for a reply to the message she had sent to London several hours earlier. Assuming the person to whom it was addressed had received it, she realised it would not be an easy decision for him to take. So far as she knew, he alone was aware of what she had been doing since Yalta in February 1945 and, moreover, aware that what she was engaged in was not only highly irregular for an operative of her background but also highly dangerous. She was risking her reputation not just out of loyalty to her service and her country, but because Sokolov intrigued her. Because he had approached her it was right that, as his putative handler, she should nurture his professed wish to pass secrets to the British government. If her departmental colleagues knew what she was doing, there would be severe criticism that a former SOE agent was recklessly performing a task far beyond her remit and ability, a task likely to jeopardise other sensitive operations. Her position was all the more precarious because, if the opportunity arose, some of her colleagues would, she knew, seize on her involvement to bring her down.

Lighting a cigarette, she reflected on the life that had brought her to this game of hazard in which she sat awaiting confirmation of her next move. Her London suburban parents had sent her – their only child – to a good girls' school, after which she read languages at university. Following graduation, she accepted a post to teach French and German in a boys' school. Soon tiring of this, she travelled, in the 1930s, through France and Germany and afterwards went with a friend to America. Unbeknown to many, she also visited Moscow, where she spent several months learning Russian. On her return to London she had met her future husband, John, a flying instructor, in a bar. A handsome, self-assured pilot with whom she instantly fell madly in love, he was prompt to propose and they married in 1938, shortly after the Munich conference. With the outbreak of war, he joined the RAF.

Not prepared to stay at home, she answered a War Office advertisement seeking applications from those good at foreign languages. After a long interview process and stringent vetting, she had been recruited into the newly formed Special Operations Executive, where she became intimately involved in the planning of operations to drop agents into occupied France. This work with its long hours and her husband's constant missions repelling German bombers over England meant they had little time together. He was shot down in the spring of 1941; never recovering from his injuries, he died at the end of the summer. She begged to go as an agent into France. Accepted and trained, she was withdrawn at the last moment for reasons that were never explained. Her withdrawal had been a bitter disappointment. Thereafter, her life had followed a pattern of long hours and dreary bedsits in London. She had enjoyed casual sexual encounters and more serious relationships but, despite several proposals of marriage, had turned each one down. In 1944, unusually, MI6 had approached her superiors about her transfer to their European operations. They agreed and, though she was sorry to leave the excitement of SOE, she looked forward to the thrill of covert activity aimed at penetrating Soviet intelligence. Out of the blue, she was asked to join the Prime Minister's delegation at the Yalta conference, ostensibly to handle inward and outward telegrams, but in reality as one of several tasked to observe Stalin's delegation to see if there might be any potential agents to recruit to British intelligence by whatever means. Apparently,

Churchill himself had considered her a good choice – at the age of thirty-five she was charming, feminine, alluring and flirtatious, though she was known by some for her sharp tongue, the very qualities that had impressed the head of MI6.

A telegram arrived. The cipher clerk shook his head – still no reply from London. She sat back and lit another cigarette. Colonel Sokolov had caught her attention shortly after the Prime Minister arrived in Yalta on 4 February 1945. She had encountered him for the first time when they passed each other in one of the many corridors of the Livadia Palace – a grand edifice built of white Crimean stone in a neo-Renaissance style, and comprising 116 rooms. Tall, slim and personable, he had stopped to ask her name and what she was doing in the delegation, complimenting en passant the Prime Minister on his choice of such an attractive woman on his personal staff. He spoke excellent English, as befitting a senior officer in Soviet military intelligence – a fact he did not disclose but which was evident from his suave manner, his appreciation of the subtleties of English humour and eyes full of amusement. His flirtatious manner increased after he discovered that the good-looking woman in a close-fitting military uniform spoke Russian.

During the next couple of days their paths crossed several times. It soon became evident to Dorothy that this was by design and she felt flattered, not least because he had clearly begun to suspect that she was not just a cipher clerk but perhaps a member of the opposing intelligence service. She noted that he watched her closely, observing where she sat in the conference room and how she was treated by those senior civil servants and defence staff close to the Prime Minister – which was respectfully. As he observed her, she observed him. Both knew they were playing the same game. His attention to her was another of the inevitable and well-known hallmarks of a senior officer in Soviet intelligence: observing relationships was a crucial aspect of judging the position and importance of individuals in a structure that might be penetrated. It was an essential part of the foreplay to an approach.

On Thursday 8 February, three days before the conference ended, she was working late in the British office when she received a message from Sokolov asking if she was free to join him for a drink – or for a night cap, as he had written. After a brief hesitation, she sent a reply advising that it would be another hour before she was free. That was not exactly true but it was important to keep him waiting, to play with his expectations. Back came Sokolov's messenger immediately with a note saying he would delay his night cap until she was able to join him. She responded – adding another fifteen minutes to his wait – that she would meet him in the palace foyer.

Over an hour and a quarter later, they met, formally shaking hands. Dorothy chose a corner near the Italian patio where they would be seen but not overheard. They chatted for more than an hour, he drinking several double vodkas, she a fruit juice chosen by her at random from a cabinet behind the bar. Each knew they were performing a predictable but elaborate choreography. He knew that she knew he was a member of Soviet military intelligence. She knew too that he had begun a long-established procedure to put her at ease in the hope that she would disclose information, however small and incidental a piece, that might give him a better foothold for eliciting further disclosures, either through enticement or eventual blackmail. His remarks were overtly flirtatious, with increasing sexual overtones as he consumed each vodka. This amused and again flattered her. Meanwhile she was playing her game, exploring his attitudes through a series of apparently innocent questions about Soviet aims in the remaining part of the war, in order to judge what scope there might be for luring him into her net. But she had to tread with great care.

She wanted to avoid any risk that he might fear his bonhomie was being repelled or that she found his behaviour boorish; equally she wanted to put him at ease and to encourage him to continue to talk to her about this and that. She understood that, for his part, he too would want to exercise care in his approach to a woman whom he clearly found physically attractive and whose attraction would be all the greater because of his suspicion that she belonged to British intelligence. He would think her quite a catch for his service. Inwardly, Dorothy was aware that in accepting the invitation to a night cap she was already exceeding her explicit instructions – which were merely to observe potential agents and to report back, nothing more than that. At the commencement of this delicate ballet, she was the ballerina waiting for her partner's first move. But he needed some enticement.

While he went to fetch more vodka, she crossed her legs, an excuse to raise the hemline of her skirt just above her knees. Her action had not gone unnoticed on his return. He edged closer to her. They continued chatting, she deploying her allure and at one point, during laughter at one of his jokes, patting his knee. He clearly liked the gesture.

By then it was almost 1.30 a.m. and after a few more minutes of friendly banter she rose, insisting it was time to leave if she were to be ready for an early start in what was already the morning. He walked with her towards the palace entrance to find a car to take her to the nearby Alupka Palace, where the British delegation was staying. On the way, he said he wanted to show her the gallery which connected the palace with the adjacent neo-Byzantine Church of the Exultation of the Cross. As they turned a corner he pulled her gently into an alcove and tried to kiss her on the mouth. She resisted, whispering in his ear, "Behave, Colonel Sokolov. Do you want your authorities to be aware of your predilection for a uniformed British woman in a short skirt? Better we go our separate ways."

The telegram machine chattered but once again it was not the message she wanted. Her thoughts turned back to Yalta.

The following day he had pressed a scribbled message into her hand. She walked on, only reading it once she reached her desk. Apologising for his behaviour the day before, he asked if they might meet later so he could say sorry in person. She tore the scrap of paper into pieces. Later, he brushed against her as they stood in a group waiting for the three leaders to emerge from their latest session. She smiled.

"I'm on an early shift this evening. What about you, Colonel? Will your master let you off early?"

He simply returned her smile, shrugging his shoulders.

That evening, out of uniform, she joined several British and

American colleagues on the waterfront, overlooking the Black Sea, for a meal. Sokolov and several other Soviet officers joined them. The party ate and drank well, though Dorothy, carefully concealing the fact, remained abstemious.

As the evening drew to a close, the restaurant emptied, with the diners walking along the seafront in groups of two or three. Sokolov, Dorothy and a young British naval officer neared the Alupka Palace. As they approached the entrance, the Prime Minister got out of his car, cigar in his mouth and evidently in good spirits after yet another duel of words with Stalin. In the hubbub, Sokolov drew Dorothy to one side to apologise for the previous evening. They walked between some tall shrubs that surrounded the palace walls. She decided that this was the moment she would exceed her instructions yet again.

"I will be sorry when you leave, Miss Dorothy."

"And I will be sorry too."

"May I kiss you?" he asked.

"Yes, of course. I would like to have the thrill of being kissed by a senior Soviet intelligence officer."

There, she had said it, and he did not demur.

"And I would like to be kissed by a British agent."

She said nothing.

They kissed, not a brush of lips but a passionate kiss in his firm embrace.

"The deed is done," said Dorothy.

"Indeed it is," he replied.

Dorothy smiled and walked away, sensing his gaze following her. As she entered her bedroom, she still tingled from the embrace of a highly intelligent schemer, from his palpable desire to seduce her. She imagined what he would be like in bed.

The final night of the conference was busy as the leaders sought to reach agreement on what would happen to Europe once the war was eventually over. After the last session, there was much *joie de vivre*. She saw Sokolov across the room. Had she successfully lured him into a corner, or had she made a terrible misjudgement that would end in her disgrace in London? She would find out.

"You look fatigued, Colonel. Has our Prime Minister been too difficult? We'll be out of your way tomorrow. Then you can all recover."

The noise in the room was loud and at first Dorothy found it difficult to hear his reply. He leaned towards her.

"I don't want you to go."

"Why is that?"

"It's been a pleasure to make your acquaintance. If only we had more time."

"Yes, it is a pity," she replied.

He tugged her arm, gently leading her away from the boisterousness.

"I wish to go to London."

"Why don't you seek a posting at your embassy? There's always room for people like you," she replied with an impish smile.

"If only it were that easy," he whispered, as a Soviet officer passed by.

"There are several ways to get to London. It may take more time. But if that's your goal I'm sure there will be people – the right people – who could make the necessary introductions."

"What could I do in London?"

"Colonel, what a silly question you ask and coming from such an accomplished man! You know the game. Just play it and see who becomes your opponent or your ally."

Sokolov smiled. "Yes, I do know the game. I will play it someday."

"You must do whatever you think is best for you."

At that point, they were joined by others.

The following morning – after one last meeting of the leaders and the final photograph for posterity – each delegation said goodbye. Sokolov, accompanied by others, came to say farewell.

"Here is a parting gift. It's a photographic reminder of Yalta."

She smiled. "Thank you, Colonel, and all of your colleagues, for your kindness."

"I hope that one day we might meet again." He shook her hand and added, in case he was being overheard, "That all of us will meet again when this war is over."

"I'm sure we will."

On the flight back to London, Dorothy removed the photograph from its envelope. It was a picture of the two of them on the Yalta waterfront framed in stiff brown board. He had signed it. She looked at the back. The cardboard inset was held in place by small adhesive strips, which looked new compared to the condition of the frame. One by one she peeled them back and lifted the inset. Tucked inside was a tightly folded square of thin paper. She slowly unfolded it. In neat small handwriting, in English, was an annotated list of Russian army deployments around Berlin. At the bottom was written in even smaller handwriting the words:

Here is a deposit towards the cost of my journey to London. I wait for your reply.

She replaced the sheet of paper, resealed the photograph and returned it to the envelope. She sat back, eyes closed, to grasp the significance of the past few days. Was this information genuine or was it a sophisticated trap? She decided that, since she was largely regarded more as an adornment at headquarters than as a valued contributor to the campaign against Soviet espionage, she would ask to see the chief on her return, an act of risk in itself. If Sokolov was to become a British agent she wanted to win the prize, to earn the credit, herself, not share it with others.

To her surprise, after a reprimand for freelancing in such an unorthodox way, contrary to her instructions, the dour almost monosyllabic Menzies agreed that she should respond to Sokolov personally. Her brief was to provide him with further opportunities to convey more sensitive information, in an effort to prove beyond doubt that he was not seeking to ensnare her. She did so, thus beginning a relationship to test the veracity of what he had said and provided in Yalta. A temporary transfer to Munich was arranged after the German surrender, for her to liaise with US army Major Max Steiner of their war crimes section, involved in tracking former Nazis. This provided good cover for her continued contact with Sokolov, passing to him by various means carefully crafted bait disclosing details of British intentions in Berlin. He passed on her information, convincing his superiors that he had entrapped a British agent, while encouraging her to produce information of more substance. The aftermath of quadripartite meetings in the Kommandatura provided further occasional opportunities for the exchange of messages, often accompanied by a surreptitious squeeze of his hand or arm to remind him of implied sexual contact to come.

The telegram machine coughed into life again but still no message from London.

She lit yet another cigarette, her nerves increasingly on edge. She recalled their infrequent moments of discreet contact in Nuremburg, away from the tribunal building and from any prying eyes in the Soviet prosecution team. Each small amount of intelligence he delivered – and each appeared credible to her – added, in her opinion, to accumulating proof that he was genuine. But conclusively testing its credibility was a matter for London, to whom she passed each piece, without stating the source. To her knowledge, the veracity of the reports she provided was never questioned. In one rendezvous, they had gone to a place of her choosing where she invited him to make love to her. He responded with alacrity. She watched his reaction as she slowly and provocatively undressed. She came quickly despite his roughness, her pleasure driven by the excitement not just of having sex with a man after so long but with a Soviet traitor. Shortly after, he was transferred back to Berlin, making it necessary to find a new means of keeping in touch. It had been her idea that Sokolov should abduct Karin Eilers from the arms of Richard Fortescue and take her to East Berlin, thus providing a pretext for continued contact. Though some of the consequences of the plan had been unforeseen, her visits to Karlshorst and her play-acting in front of the Russians provided a good alibi for her to pass more made-up Foreign Office information to him and for him to respond with reports of his own. But she fretted increasingly that this channel under Russian noses might somehow leak beyond the one man in London.

The black book had been an unexpected complication. Again she ran through its implications, on which her current plans were predicated. If Fortescue was right in his assertion that it contained Sokolov's name – perhaps because he had been in touch with the German intelligence network during the earlier part of the war – it was possible that he was already known at her headquarters in London, as British intelligence had penetrated the *Abwehr* at that time. If that were the case, and there was indeed a Soviet agent in the Broadway hierarchy as some rumours were already suggesting, it was conceivable that Sokolov may already have been compromised in Moscow and that his superiors were allowing him sufficient rope to penetrate more of MI6 before they disposed of him. If that were so, it was urgent to warn him to get out before he was unmasked and snuffed out by Moscow – and to secure the release of Karin Eilers at the same time. It was the least she could do, having placed her in Russian hands.

The machine clattered, delivering a fresh telegram from London. She waited. A few minutes later the cipher clerk placed a short unsigned message on her desk.

Yes. Extreme vigilance.

The next day the British sent a message to the Russian command in East Berlin informing them that, in accordance with an earlier understanding, Mrs Maddox intended once again to visit the prisoner, Karin Eilers, who had been removed without authorisation from the British sector. Within two days, back came the reply instructing Dorothy to come to Karlshorst on the afternoon of Thursday 24 April, when she should report to Colonel Sokolov. Dorothy knew that by going she was once again placing herself in extreme danger. If Sokolov had been betrayed, she might be arrested and put on trial in a Russian court or persuaded to betray her country to save her life.

* * * * *

Helga Eilers became restless in custody. After prolonged cowardice following Germany's collapse, she had at last summoned the courage to surrender her freedom, restricted though it had been during her self-imposed incarceration in Grunewald and, more briefly, Spandau. She had decided she would face with pride the close questioning of her actions and motives, just as many she had known had faced interrogation and trial at Nuremburg. As each day passed and no one came to interview her, her sense of self-importance started to evaporate, while her regret that she had cast the trinkets of her past into the river increased. It began to cross her mind that perhaps she had already been forgotten, that her sins were too unimportant, not worth the effort of prosecution because she had become an irrelevant relic.

Languishing in her locked room, she was unaware of the debate within British headquarters in London and in the Berlin intelligence office whether to let her go or to make her available to the Russians, who regularly demanded her transfer, though their motives were as opaque to outsiders as ever. No conclusion was reached, other than that she would remain in custody pending the completion of further enquiries, a euphemism for doing nothing in the hope that someone else would provide the answer.

A few days later the US army war crimes section passed to British headquarters a communication they had received about Helga Eilers from a Jewish source. The source claimed it had certain information about the detainee, alleging her close association with senior SS personnel involved with concentration camp operations. While her role may have been more incidental than direct, this new information warranted further investigation before her release could be considered.

Receiving a copy of the US message, Dorothy Maddox followed it up. The information seemed to point to Helga Eilers's possible involvement in making arrangements for the transport of Jewish families to the East, and in preparing reports for Himmler and others more directly involved in the so-called final solution. In Dorothy's opinion, the evidence the war crimes section had provided was thin but, combined with other material, the allegations were of sufficient strength to enable her to pass them to Sokolov so he could again demonstrate to his superiors that he was receiving information from a potential key British intelligence source he was carefully and slowly nurturing. This might help to deflect any suspicion that he had become a British agent.

* * * * *

Dorothy Maddox's frequent contacts with Colonel Sokolov and the direct channel she apparently had to the highest echelon in London irritated Charles Nolan, given his role as the official in charge of the steadily expanding British intelligence station in Berlin. A long-standing servant of the Crown, first as a member of the police force and now as an MI6 intelligence officer, he regarded her as an interfering woman of junior rank acting outside the established and accepted line of control. He could not understand – or indeed tolerate – why she should be devoting precious time to the fate of a young German woman with whom an equally young, albeit highly regarded British officer had stupidly become infatuated, leading him to some foolhardy actions and damaging his career. Nor could he understand why she seemed to be bypassing her immediate superiors and dealing direct with the very top in London. Finally losing his patience, he had gone to the British Commandant and to his Foreign Office advisers to vent his frustration, thus breaching the convention of not discussing intelligence matters with outsiders. The Commandant had, as Nolan predicted, expressed his displeasure and taken the matter up with the War Office in London, who in turn had contacted the Foreign Office. A few days later Nolan received a reprimand for disclosing sensitive information to the Commandant and for questioning Mrs Maddox's activities and, moreover, her loyalty.

Nolan's gripe about her had also reached the attention of the well-regarded British agent, Kim Philby, who had recently been appointed head of British intelligence in Turkey. It had reached him via Donald Maclean in the Foreign Office. Philby followed closely MI6 efforts to penetrate Soviet intelligence in Berlin. Any information about Soviet contacts was therefore always worth reading. He was curious about the apparent regular contacts with Sokolov in Berlin but was unable to find out more.

At the same time, a message from her US counterpart, Major Max Steiner, gave Dorothy Maddox additional cause for alarm. It reported the view in one quarter of the CIA that the Russians had already penetrated her service in London, though no one knew the identity of the traitor. Dorothy decided that, with the implicit support of her chief, it was now essential to warn Sokolov that he was possibly at great risk of being unmasked and that he should immediately seek sanctuary in the West – bringing Karin Eilers at the same time. There could be no further delay.

* * * * *

Colonel Julian Phillips, previously part of the British prosecution team at Nuremburg, flew to Berlin at the War Office's request to question Helga Eilers and to persuade Richard Fortescue to reveal the whereabouts of the black book. He chose to speak to Fortescue first.

"Richard, tell me, how have you got yourself into this mess? You're under arrest, awaiting court-martial for allegedly killing a German national, which you insist was in self-defence, while at the same time you're in a relationship with a young German woman who's now in Soviet hands and whose mother was part of the Nazi bureaucracy. What's more, you've apparently got a notebook that, according to you, contains a list of names prepared for Himmler, which you won't hand over. And you've lost your fiancée. When you could have been in London pursuing a legal career on the back of your reputation in Nuremburg and getting married to a general's daughter! That's rather a mess, wouldn't you agree? And I certainly wouldn't trust Mrs Maddox, to whom you confided the shooting. She gave you a bullet to replace the one you fired in Seeshaupt and then she shopped you. I have never trusted MI6 – an encounter with them is a kiss of death for anyone, I would have thought. So tell me, what the hell is really going on? You must tell me, if you want my help."

Fortescue shrugged his shoulders.

"Don't be bloody stupid, man. You and I worked together in Nuremburg. You will be a fine lawyer one day – but only if you see sense. I believe in your innocence and I will do all that I can to get you a fair trial and exoneration. But I need your trust. I need you to tell me the truth. I'm not here acting on behalf of British intelligence. In short, I want you on my staff in London, not stuck here. And I couldn't give a damn about your affection for the German girl you picked up in Munich. Now, Richard, where is the book? Tell me where it is and I can start to secure your freedom."

Fortescue had known Phillips since before Nuremburg, a good army lawyer whose judgement, honesty, principles and commitment to seeking the truth without fear or favour he respected. They talked well into the evening, testing each other. Shortly before midnight, Fortescue made up his mind. He would after all place his trust in Phillips. He reached for the volume of Shakespeare, opened it, removed the well-thumbed black book and after an almost imperceptible hesitation passed it across the table.

"Julian, I trust you to use this book to uncover the truth – why I have been so badly misused – and to use it also to secure Karin's freedom. She has been caught up in this blatant fabrication through no fault of her own. She deserves her freedom. I owe that to her and so do those responsible for putting her in a Soviet jail. If you break my trust, I will never forgive you. I will regard you as my enemy."

Phillips leaned across the table.

"The pursuit of justice has always been my overriding objective. It matches my unquenchable patriotism. You have my word. But let me say this in return. If I find that you have lied to me, I will never again hold you in high esteem."

They shook hands.

"By the way, you're a cheeky bugger – keeping the book with you under the noses of the RMPs while they have been searching high and low for it elsewhere. I take my hat off to you. I would never have thought of that."

Fortescue smiled.

* * * * *

There was little appetite in British headquarters for keeping Helga Eilers much longer. Her presence was a distraction. The inclination was to let her go or to hand her to the Americans and let them deal with the Russians. But it was agreed at the urging of the intelligence office that Colonel Phillips should question her in the light of the information the US army war crimes section had provided. Two days after his long conversation with Fortescue, Phillips began his interrogation. Though he had listened to the harrowing evidence of female victims at Nuremburg, he had interrogated few women during his army legal career. He would proceed with forensic care and civility. She could not be bullied. If she had a hidden past, she must condemn herself.

Helga Eilers sat opposite him, plainly dressed, her hair well brushed. The trace of make-up she wore could not conceal the unhealthy pallor and heavy lines of her face; her eyes were fatigued and her cheekbones revealed a significant loss of weight, no longer the striking woman his research confirmed she had once been. Yet despite all that had happened to her since her escape from the bunker, she conveyed confidence, an air of resolve, seeming ready to defend with conviction whatever principles she espoused. Her interrogator would test the depth of her resolve.

"Tell me, Frau Eilers, about your early life. Set the scene for me."

"How much do you wish to know, Colonel? My early life was ordinary."

"Let me be the judge of that," Phillips replied.

She described her childhood, growing up in a poor household and her decision to become a teacher of children aged five to ten. Encouraged to continue her story, she spoke about her unhappy marriage, her husband's decision to join the

Brownshirts and his murder by the SS in 1934, her struggle to give her husband's son and her daughter an education and her strong wish to better her life. The Nazi Party had spoken of the creation of a strong and powerful nation. This aim had appealed to her because, having little money to spare, she thought that supporting the cause might provide the chance to earn more, to show what she could do.

"Is that the reason you became a Party member – not just an ordinary member but a member ready to show commitment, to help make a difference?"

"Yes. Like many women I was captivated by the Führer, by his promises and by his magnetism. I met him once at a rally. I shook his hand as he walked past. He was different."

"But the SS murdered your husband and many other Brownshirts on orders from the very top. Why should you join such a party of killers and work hard for them?"

She paused before answering.

"I worked hard for the Party because I believed in the Führer. For my neighbours and friends and me, he was our leader. He convinced me that if I served the Party I would enjoy a better life."

"And did you?" asked Phillips.

"Yes," she replied, her eyes suddenly becoming alive.

"Tell me."

She described how she had devoted more and more time to Party affairs in her district of Berlin, what fun it had become. Then, out of the blue, she had been asked to work temporarily in the Propaganda Ministry, working on the Party newspaper. She was asked to write an article, and much to her surprise and pleasure it was accepted and published. Goebbels had praised her and arranged for her to become a paid employee at the Ministry. Life became financially easier and she began to meet some of the top people in the Party.

"Was it really fun, Frau Eilers?"

"Yes, it was," she said with a smile. "I had become somebody important. I knew more than others. I enjoyed the thrill of it all. And then I was appointed to the Minister's personal staff. Much more information passed across my desk. I knew more about what was going on. And I had even more social invitations."

"What did you do in the Ministry?"

"Typing, organising meetings, making notes, ensuring that people did what they said they would do – that is what I did," she said with evident pride and self-satisfaction.

"Were there more rewards?" he asked.

"Yes," she replied.

"Tell me about some of them."

"There were more invitations – special invitations, to the Reich Chancellery and once or twice to the Berghof."

"Was that all?" Phillips enquired.

"That was all," she replied, growing nervous as she became aware of the drift of his more penetrating questions.

"Are you sure? Or was there more – ingratiating yourself with the top people by offering yourself for sex? The more sex you provided, the more you got in rewards. And was it not the case you became well-known in the upper echelons of the SS? Perhaps it was because of the services you offered?"

"No, that is not true! It was not like that at all. I just helped where I could. They were good men. I respected them and they respected me. The Führer told me so."

"And you took his word for it."

"Yes, I did," she asserted. Her face turned even paler. She lit a cigarette to calm her nerves. She realised she had gone too far, spoken too vehemently.

"Frau Eilers, you have told me your story in great detail. I welcome that, because it has revealed your character. Because of your love for the Party, you lost your moral compass, abandoned any care for your son and daughter, and indulged your weakness for moral depravity and lust – not so much for the pleasure of sex with powerful men, though I am sure that was a factor, but a lust to be part of a hideous ideology. An admirer of those eventually found guilty at Nuremburg of the most hideous of crimes, you turned a blind eye. You had come from a deprived background. Now people respected and envied you for mixing with those in Hitler's inner circle."

"No, it wasn't like that. I loved my children and did my best to give them a good upbringing. But it was hard. The only way I could help them was to work for the Party. I did my best and, though I now see many of the things they did were bad, they cared for me. I was one of thousands of German women who believed in the Führer."

"But you went further. You not only believed in the Führer and the philosophy the Party spouted, you used it for your own purposes whatever the personal cost – to you and others – and even though you knew what the Nazis were doing."

"No, it was not like that. It just wasn't," she insisted again, shaking her head.

Phillips paused to allow her to compose herself, before reaching across for a large cardboard box. He placed it in front of her and removed the lid.

"Here are some of the contents of the case you threw into the river on the day you gave yourself up. Now let's have a look, shall we?"

One by one, he took out each item and placed it on the table: the signed and grandly framed picture of the man she had served; the diamond swastika pendant; the ring; and some correspondence, which he unfolded.

"What do you have to say to these baubles of corruption? And what have you to say about this letter – apparently from Reinhard Heydrich, thanking you for the material you had helped to prepare for his Wannsee conference on the 20th of January 1942 concerning procedures for the extermination of Jews in the East? What friends you had and what trust was placed in you! You were no ordinary secretary. You had become an official and a Party prostitute."

She crumpled, her mouth unable to utter any words.

From beneath the table, Phillips produced her handbag, flourishing it like a rabbit out of a hat.

"Who gave you this handbag?"

Helga stumbled over the name.

"I didn't hear you. Who gave it to you?"

"Frau Goebbels, shortly before the end," she stammered.

"Among this correspondence there is a letter from her, giving you the bag as a gift, a precious reward for service to her husband."

Helga nodded.

"Did you ever examine the bag?"

"No," she replied.

"We have. Inside – in this concealed pocket – is a piece of paper and a ticket. On the piece of paper is written an address here in Berlin, where an object can be found awaiting collection in return for the ticket. We have been to the address. Despite the damage to the building we found the object – a fifteenth-century triptych of the life of Mary, the mother of Christ. The triptych – stolen from an art collection in Poland – was meant for you. That was the precious reward for your loyalty. So, instead of shivering in the cold in Berlin since the end of the war, you could have collected this picture, sold it and bought yourself a new life somewhere far away from the country that the people you idolised wrecked. But you didn't because you didn't look. You just kept the bag for sentimental reasons. The result is that we've found the stolen art and we will return it."

She buried her face in her hands.

"What have you to say?"

She said nothing.

"Frau Eilers, we will shortly decide what should happen to you. Whether you should be handed to the German authorities in respect of your evident connivance with certain senior Nazi officials in actions tantamount to war crimes and for the possession of stolen art, or whether we should accede to a request from the Soviet authorities, who wish to question you on other matters."

As she was led away sobbing, she begged not to be handed to the Russians.

"If you are handed to them, you will be able to join your daughter, whom they are holding on a spurious charge."

Later that day, Phillips reported his recommendation, which was that Helga Eilers be passed to the German authorities in the West. He added that it was his intention to press for the charges against Major Fortescue to be dropped on the grounds of insufficient evidence and the likelihood that he was an innocent victim in a wider plot involving national security. He would use the black book now in his possession to substantiate his case.

* * * * *

In East Berlin, Karin Eilers prepared as best she could for her forthcoming trial for alleged murder in a Soviet military court. The scene would be set for the final denouement of her fate and others'.

CHAPTER THIRTEEN

The Endgame

Dorothy Maddox had prepared meticulously for her appointment in Karlshorst. Though she had done the journey before, it was still necessary to ensure everything was in order each time, as she had done so often in the SOE, preparing agents for drops over occupied France. Trusting only herself, everything had to be checked and rechecked – those things she would take with her and those she would leave behind. Crossing into the Soviet sector had become even riskier, each day more uncertain than the one before.

There could be no mistake, no slip-up. Too much was at stake. Russian unpredictability and blatant antagonism made daily life increasingly difficult for the three Western Allies, particularly as the Soviet noose restricting road access to the western part of the city grew steadily tighter. The tense situation was frequently inflamed by misunderstandings and misjudgements on both sides. As the relationship steadily deteriorated, the British authorities rigidly enforced the rule that intelligence officers should not enter the eastern sector of Berlin for fear of possible abduction. Contrary to this instruction, Dorothy was going to meet Colonel Sokolov and doing so alone.

She had paid equally scrupulous attention to her appearance and was dressed smartly in a black coat over a dark close-fitting skirt, its hem just above the knee, with a matching jacket, and wearing high heels. After a last look at herself in the mirror to adjust her beret, and checking once more that there was no ladder in her stockings, she closed the door behind her. She got into the waiting car, carefully placing her expensive black-leather handbag beside her, and signalled to the driver. He slowly pulled away for the city centre. She noticed his expression as he glimpsed at her in his rear-view mirror, and smiled to herself, imagining how she might appear to him: perhaps like a femme fatale, about to step onto a film set – unemotional, self-confident and deadly.

It took over half an hour to reach the sector boundary. She got out, showed her laissez-passer to the British military police guard, doing a routine check. Declining to exchange pleasantries, she told the driver who had brought her that she was now going to cross on foot. He should not wait for her as she didn't know how long she would be. She walked across the line into the Soviet sector without looking back towards the West. The guards, a mixture of Russians and East Germans, made no attempt to look at her papers. At the foot of Friedrichstraße, she saw the familiar large black Soviet limousine waiting for her, its engine running. As she approached, the uniformed driver got out, saluted her and opened the rear door.

"Thank you, Corporal," she said in flawless Russian.

"It's good to see you again. The Colonel awaits your arrival with great anticipation."

"I'm sure he does. Let's go, so that he does not become too impatient."

As the vehicle turned right at the intersection with the Unter den Linden, Dorothy looked to the left at the distant silhouette of the Brandenburg Gate, wondering if she would ever see it again.

* * * * *

At British military police headquarters the telephone rang. It was Charles Nolan, asking to speak to the duty sergeant.

"I've been trying to reach Mrs Maddox. I believe she intends to cross into the Soviet sector later. Ask your patrols to look out for her. When they make contact, they should tell her to phone me before she goes across. It's urgent."

"I'm afraid you've missed her, Sir. She crossed into the Russian sector some time ago according to our men, who checked her papers. She sent her driver away as she no longer had need for him. He has now returned to headquarters."

Nolan swore.

"Is there anything you wish me to do?" asked the sergeant.

"Please call me the moment that bloody woman reappears. If she refuses, arrest her."

"Yes, Sir," the sergeant replied.

Nolan sat back in his chair. She had broken all the rules. Yet in his hand was a copy of a message from the top echelon at London headquarters appearing to authorise her journey. There was nothing he could do – at least not for now – apart from recording his personal disapproval of the high-handed way in which she had behaved. If it all went wrong, he would make sure no blame accrued to him.

* * * * *

Major-General Eric Paytherus Nares, previously of the Cheshire Regiment, had arrived in Berlin to take up the post of Commandant on 30 August 1945. He had fought in the First World War, was wounded twice and had been awarded the Military Cross with bar. In the recent war, he had served in the Middle East, North Africa and the Mediterranean. An impressive but quietly spoken man, he sat one side of the large conference table in his office at Lancaster House. His Chief of Staff, Colonel Paycock, sat on his right and Alexander Blackstone, from the Foreign Office liaison team, on his left. His visitors faced them.

"Colonel Phillips, I invite you to make your submission concerning Major Richard Fortescue. The Major is shortly due for court-martial but I understand from Colonel Paycock that before the process begins you wish to bring to our attention certain matters arising from your close examination – if I may use that term – of some facts that have come to light."

"Thank you, Major-General. I am grateful for this opportunity. With Colonel Paycock's permission, I recently interviewed Major Fortescue at length to hear his account of the events that have led to his predicament and to put certain questions to him. I will not be his defence in the forthcoming court-martial. That is the responsibility of Major Petworth, on my left, who agreed, as did Major Fortescue, to the action I took. You are indeed correct that new information has come to light from the Major's answers to my questions. He also handed me a notebook in his possession, which has been the subject of an intensive search by the military police. Before I proceed further, do you have any questions, Major-General, as to my locus in this matter?"

"I have none, Colonel Phillips. Please go ahead."

"Major Fortescue was part of the British prosecution team at Nuremburg. He was interviewed extensively during the selection process in order to judge his suitability for the interrogation of certain defendants. His German-language skill was of the highest standard and his commitment and impartiality were considered second to none. Our chief prosecutor, Sir Hartley Shawcross, personally approved his selection. Major Fortescue conducted himself at Nuremburg in full compliance with the tribunal's principles and procedures. His work led to the preparation of strong cases against several of those indicted. I have here – in this file – copies of written reports of his work. They point to exemplary behaviour, sound judgement and strong character."

Phillips pushed the folder towards the Commandant.

"Thank you, Colonel. My Chief of Staff has already briefed me on their content. I have no questions about them. Please continue."

"Following the tribunal's verdicts of last October and the subsequent execution of those sentenced to death, Major Fortescue received notice that he should return to London in order to be interviewed about the continuation of his army career. While Sir Hartley had indicated that he hoped the Major would also consider a career at the bar, we in the War Office hoped that he would remain. Another reason for his return to London was his anticipated engagement to Miss Susannah Thomas, General Thomas's daughter. Major Fortescue was aware of these career possibilities but before making arrangements to fly to London he decided to stay a few days in Munich, a city he had visited before the war.

"It was while he was in Munich that he met two women who feature in this case. The first was Mrs Dorothy Maddox, a member of British intelligence, who was supposedly in the city for liaison with the US army war crimes unit. The second was Fräulein Karin Eilers, daughter of Frau Helga Eilers, once on the staff of Joseph Goebbels. Major Fortescue and Fräulein Eilers met by chance in a coffee bar one morning. She accepted an invitation to join him at the opera that night. Afterwards, he escorted her back to her apartment block with the intention of saying goodnight and then returning to his accommodation. As he left, he heard a scuffle on the landing above. He went upstairs and found a man attempting to rape her. He fought off the young woman's assailant. As she was deeply distressed, he took her back to his accommodation, informing Mrs Maddox of her presence. A taxi driver who took them from the opera to the apartment block and back to where he was staying has provided a witness statement to corroborate this account.

"The following day they went back to the apartment block. The door to the flat in which she had been living was open. Inside, they found the bodies of two people who had been brutally murdered. Details are in this folder. One of the victims was the young woman in whose name the flat was rented. The other was Fräulein Eilers's brother, Gerhard, who had also been staying there. They did not linger, only long enough for Fräulein Eilers to remove a notebook from its hiding place. According to the Fräulein, the book, which was marked inside for the personal attention of Himmler, was all that was left of certain documents that acquaintances of her mother had deposited at the flat for safe keeping towards the end of the war. These were subsequently stolen by persons unknown. The book, the last item to be taken to the flat and described by the person who brought it as particularly valuable and sensitive, had been concealed by her friend in a different place from the other documents. Without interfering with the crime scene, they quickly left in the same taxi that had brought them. I have a copy of the taxi driver's testimony."

"Major Fortescue should have reported what he and the Fräulein had seen. They did not. That was a serious error of judgement on his part."

"I agree, Colonel Paycock," Phillips replied. "And he made other misjudgements too. He went with Fräulein Eilers to Seeshaupt without disclosing he was doing so. While it was undesirable, at the very least, to enter into a physical relationship with her, it soon became clear to him that her mother was on a list of Nazi officials still wanted for questioning. Third, it is alleged by the Munich police that he shot and killed an unarmed man, with his army pistol, in the forest surrounding Seeshaupt, thus making Fräulein Eilers an accomplice to alleged murder. Major Fortescue claims that the man was armed and approached him and Fräulein Eilers with the intention of harming them. He said he fired in self-defence. A yet further error was that he did not immediately report what had happened. However, he did later confide in Mrs Maddox, who assured him all would be well. She went so far as to provide him with a bullet to replace the one he had fired so that, if questioned, he could claim he had not used his pistol. I have spoken to Detective Hessler of the Munich police who earlier interviewed Major Fortescue here in Berlin. From new information not made available earlier, it appears the detective failed to disclose that the unknown man in the forest was in fact armed and that one shot had been discharged from the weapon he possessed, though when it was fired is not clear. The weapon carried the dead man's fingerprints, and no trace of Major Fortescue's.

"So, Colonel Paycock, Major Fortescue showed more than one serious error of judgement, as he readily admitted to me. In hindsight, he wishes he had acted differently. But he was fatigued and his head had been turned by an attractive young woman. Whether he set out to seduce her or she him is hard to say. But the fact remains that, despite his failures, the circumstances of this case are not as they appear at first sight."

"Nonetheless," interjected Alexander Blackstone, "it would appear, Colonel Phillips, that, however you may wish to present the facts, Major Fortescue shot dead a German national and therefore has a case to answer."

"That would have been my prima facie conclusion too," Phillips replied. "But after questioning Major Fortescue at length, and in the light of the enquiries Major Petworth and I have made, I have concluded there was another hand at work in this matter."

"And whose might that be?" the Commandant asked.

"I believe it was an agent or agents of British intelligence."

"Why would they be involved as you have alleged?" countered the Commandant.

With a somewhat theatrical flourish, Phillips produced the black book from his briefcase, placing it on the table in front of him, the silver embossed SS symbol catching everyone's attention in the afternoon sunlight penetrating through the window.

"Major Fortescue told Mrs Maddox, the other woman who features in this case, of the notebook's existence and its potential significance – its coded contents possibly comprising a list of names and numbers, perhaps other information. Mrs Maddox expressed immediate interest and asked to see the book. Major Fortescue, much to Mrs Maddox's evident disappointment and irritation, declined, preferring to keep the book himself on the grounds that it belonged to Fräulein Eilers. Again, his judgement was questionable, given the Allied wish to evaluate all Nazi documentation, not least SS documents. But he would not be the first Allied soldier to retain a war memento."

The Commandant interrupted. "Colonel, you are persuasive in the presentation of your case but I'm afraid I do not see the link between Mrs Maddox's professed curiosity about the notebook – whatever it might contain – and Major Fortescue's alleged shooting of a man, whether in self-defence or otherwise, in the woods above Seeshaupt. Perhaps you could elaborate what you think the connection is?"

"Commandant, it is my proposition, far-fetched though it may initially sound, that two groups of people were intent on getting hold of the notebook, and indeed the other documents that had been deposited at the flat in Munich. The first group were, I submit, in all likelihood ex-Nazis seeking possession of the files and the notebook either because they revealed certain crimes that had to be covered up to avoid prosecution, or because they contained information on the whereabouts of certain items of plunder – art or other precious items, for example – which could be useful sources of much-needed money to finance the escape of war criminals. The second group, I suggest, were Allied agents, interested because of the possibility that the documentation might, if rumours were correct, contain sensitive information either about foreign sources of *Abwehr* intelligence during the war, or German military weapons secrets, which the Allies would wish to have rather than see them in Russian hands. If my latter theory is correct, it is conceivable that the man Major Fortescue shot in the forest was a Russian agent."

"How would Allied agents have known about the existence of the documents to which you have referred?" Colonel Paycock asked.

"Major Steiner of the US army war crimes section has told me that the flat where the murders took place had already been under surveillance for some time as part of their effort to locate Frau Helga Eilers, whom they wished to interview on account of her relationship with certain high-ranking SS officers and rumours of secret documents. They observed various people coming and going immediately after the end of the war but in the end did not follow up because of the necessity to concentrate on more pressing priorities. As a result, those whom the Americans believed committed the murders at the flat have eluded arrest. That unfortunate fact apart, Major Steiner said his people were aware from the Munich police that the documents and the notebook had disappeared. He had shared his frustration about their disappearance with Mrs Maddox, who later revealed to him that Major Fortescue had the book. She promised to do her best to get hold of it, so she could see exactly what information it contained. Moreover, Mr Pritchett, formerly part of the British security detail at Nuremburg, sent a message to British intelligence that he believed Major Fortescue's motives for returning to Berlin were suspicious."

There was silence. The Commandant looked at the papers in front of him. Blackstone looked at Phillips.

"I put it to you, Commandant, on the basis of supposition, that it was agents of British intelligence, with the knowledge and possible connivance of US agents, who conceived a plan to pursue Major Fortescue and his German girlfriend, in order to get hold of the notebook because of the information it might contain and to neutralise any Soviet agents' efforts to get it first. One such Russian agent was a man called Kellerman, a Communist sympathiser, who approached Major Fortescue in Nuremburg one evening and who was subsequently murdered an hour or so later in St Sebaldus Church – possibly by US agents."

"What conclusion are you asking the Commandant to draw from this extraordinary theory you have given us today?" Blackstone asked.

"Mr Blackstone, my proposition is that, while Major Fortescue may have committed serious errors of personal judgement because of his infatuation with a young German woman, he had become – unknown to him – a pawn in a wider game being played by British and US intelligence on one side and the Soviets on the other. Yes, Major Fortescue may have fired his gun and killed a man. Or perhaps he only wounded him, and someone else used the man's gun to finish him off so he would not be tempted to divulge what had happened and whom he represented. Whichever the sequence of events, it conveniently provided a dead body to lay at Major Fortescue's door. It is my submission that, whatever the circumstances, he should not be court-martialled but exonerated and released."

"The problem, Colonel Phillips, is that there is no corroboration for your proposition – certainly concerning our intelligence people."

"I beg to differ, Mr Blackstone. Mr Nolan considers there may be grounds for intelligence to provide some clarification.

But the person best able to do so is Mrs Maddox – who, I believe, has made frequent visits to the eastern sector of the city to visit Fräulein Eilers. Miss Eilers is now facing trial for the attempted murder of a Soviet officer, following her abduction – with apparent ease, it has been noted – from the British sector by the Russians. Mrs Maddox's host has been Colonel Sokolov of Soviet military intelligence, whom she met during the Yalta conference. I am not based in Berlin but the information I have been given suggests that it is distinctly odd for a British intelligence officer to be making frequent visits on the grounds of seeking Fräulein Eilers's release. Perhaps MI6 feels it carries some responsibility for her present predicament, arising from a plan of theirs that went wrong."

Before the Commandant could speak, Blackstone interjected to propose the meeting adjourn for a few minutes. It would be in everyone's interest to do so. It was also necessary for him to make an urgent phone call. Despite some evident irritation on his part, Major-General Nares agreed. Phillips and Major Petworth gave their approval, sensing a possible change of tack. The meeting adjourned.

In the Commandant's office, Blackstone asked if he could call Charles Nolan.

"If you must, Blackstone, but don't take too long. I am anxious to get quickly to the bottom of this affair. It's dragged on far too long."

Blackstone called Nolan on the secure phone line to summarise the points Phillips had made. From the expression on Blackstone's face, the Commandant concluded that Nolan must have given him a robust reply.

"Well, what did Nolan say?"

"He asked that you terminate the meeting immediately."

"On what grounds?" the Commandant replied sharply.

"The matter raised by Colonel Phillips concerning Mrs Maddox is highly sensitive and should not be discussed."

"But that is absurd," countered the Major-General. "Major Fortescue is a good soldier and he cannot be left to languish in confinement because an allegation of MI6 involvement cannot be discussed. Let me speak to Nolan myself."

"I don't think that will serve any useful purpose. Mr Nolan has received specific instructions that because of the great sensitivity of this matter, Major Fortescue should be immediately released from custody but ordered to remain in Berlin pending a final decision."

"And when might that be?"

"Soon," Blackstone replied.

The meeting resumed, enabling the Commandant to explain what had been decided. Phillips pressed for further information but it was evident none would be forthcoming. The participants rose and left.

Later that afternoon, Fortescue was released. He joined Phillips and Petworth for supper. While they were eating, Phillips received a message that Helga Eilers had been taken to the British military hospital suffering with apparent poisoning from a leaking phial of cyanide concealed in her body. The hospital said it was too early to say whether she would survive.

* * * * *

Karin Eilers had remained in solitary confinement for several weeks, watched carefully by brutal female warders who had little sympathy for the daughter of a Nazi. Sokolov would occasionally visit her and Kovalev came sometimes to peer through the grill and to warn her that she would soon get her comeuppance. Finally, the day of her trial arrived.

It was a summary procedure. She sat handcuffed on a rough wooden bench wearing the trousers and shirt she had worn almost every day. Her hair had been cropped short. The prosecutor, ill-tempered and menacing, stated – stopping periodically so that his words could be translated into German – that she had tried to escape while being questioned by Comrade Major Kovalev. During his attempt to restrain her, she had pulled the gun from his belt and shot him. He then called Kovalev to give his evidence. He described her as a vicious inmate who had reacted violently to his persistent questions about her mother. She had suddenly lunged at him and pulled the gun from the holster, firing at him in the lower abdomen.

For a moment at the end of his evidence, the accuser turned towards the prisoner. His face displayed his contempt for her, fuelled not only by his perception that Colonel Sokolov had shown her favourable partiality but also by the shame of having his account of what happened challenged by a German prostitute. After all, it had been a German soldier who shot his father while he lay wounded on the battlefield in the East. Such an unforgivable action removed any right she had to even a modicum of human dignity.

She stared at him. All she could see beyond his hate-filled face was the ice in his heart, so manifest in his testimony of lies. The depth of his mendacity matched the bitter, unrelenting cold through which she had trudged to the court building from her cell.

After a brief and weak intervention by Major Morozov on her behalf, the judge asked the prisoner whether she wished to speak in her own defence. Watched by Sokolov, she said she wanted to make three points.

"First, I have been brought under duress to the eastern part of the city against my will. Second, Major Kovalev's statement is untrue. He attempted to rape me. I resisted. He drew his gun and threatened to shoot me if I did not acquiesce. I refused. He tried again to force himself on me, waving his pistol in front of my face. I continued to resist him. As we fought, it went off. I have never used such a weapon before. It was he, not me, who released the safety catch. Third, I am entirely innocent of the charge against me. I am a victim of the hatred of the Russian army towards the German people. But not all German people were Nazis or Nazi sympathisers. I certainly am not one of them. If I am found guilty, I will suffer my fate whatever it may be. For me, this day will record the injustice of the Soviet Union."

She sat down, her face contorted with pain, anger and fear. The judge ordered her to her feet.

"This court finds the prisoner guilty of the attempted murder of Comrade Major Kovalev and hereby sentences her to twenty years' hard labour for her actions and lack of respect for Soviet justice. Remove the prisoner."

Sokolov watched impassively as she was led back to her cell. As she disappeared from sight, he knew he had little time left to implement his plan and perhaps save her. In the labour camp, she would not survive the conditions for long.

* * * * *

On arrival at Karlshorst, Dorothy Maddox was escorted to an office on the second floor. It was damp and dingy with barred windows. She sat down at the table, placing her handbag at her feet. Watched by her escort standing close to the door, she wondered how many might have been interrogated in this room – by the Russians and the Nazis before them – and the methods used. A quarter of an hour elapsed. She asked the escort to pass a message to Colonel Sokolov that, if he had been unavoidably detained, she would return another day. He replied that the Colonel would be with her shortly.

Sokolov arrived and, amidst profuse apologies, sat down at the other side of the table. A junior officer joined him.

"Mrs Maddox, thank you for coming. I have asked Major Pavlenko to join us so he can brief you on the outcome of the trial of Fräulein Eilers. Please, Major, proceed."

Pavlenko read from what was obviously a prepared statement.

"Following a short trial lasting two hours and after due consideration of all the facts, Fräulein Eilers was found guilty of attempted murder and sentenced to twenty years' hard labour in the fatherland. Upon completion of her sentence she will be released and able to leave the Soviet Union."

Pavlenko closed the slim folder and prepared to leave. Sokolov placed a restraining hand on his arm. Dorothy concluded that he had made his first move on the board. It was now her turn.

"Colonel Sokolov, the trial and the sentence passed are illegal and unjust under Allied occupying law. Karin Eilers was abducted from the British sector without authorisation and on spurious grounds. I shall recommend to my superiors that this matter be raised at the most senior level in the Kommandatura and, if necessary, between our two governments. Such autocratic actions have no part to play if we are to restore lasting peace in Germany."

Pavlenko was writing furiously as she spoke.

"Mrs Maddox," replied Sokolov almost casually and with a slight smile, "you must recommend whatever you think best. But our position is clear. The girl will leave shortly for Siberia. The matter is now out of my hands. There is nothing I can add or do."

"So be it, Colonel," Dorothy said acidly. "May I see her?"

"No, you may not," answered Sokolov, a half smile still evident.

"In that case, there is no further point in this meeting. I will return to British headquarters and report accordingly."

"Mrs Maddox, if this is your last visit may I offer you a little Russian farewell hospitality to send you on your way? After all, our acquaintance goes back to Yalta, does it not?"

Dorothy studied his smirking face. This was his second move – in front of a witness, Pavlenko, who was no doubt an intelligence officer. She did not reply.

"Please, Mrs Maddox. Just a little drink before you leave."

She still did not reply, continuing to keep him waiting for her answer.

"Please, for old times' sake," he asked again, placing his hands together in a gesture of prayer.

"Since you insist, I will," she said. "But I do so without prejudice to what I have said I will do on my return to headquarters."

"Quite understood," Sokolov replied.

The three left the room for the main entrance.

"Pavlenko, fetch the car. We will go to the bar on the far side of the base."

The bar turned out to be a depressing ground-floor room in what had probably once been a *Wehrmacht* regimental barracks. It was unoccupied apart from a dozy, unshaven barman slouched in a chair in the corner. Sokolov gave him a kick and ordered a bottle of vodka and some water. He sat down at a rickety table, Dorothy opposite him and Pavlenko three tables away. Sokolov poured three drinks into some dirty glasses. Into one he sprinkled a substance that quickly dissolved and, winking at Dorothy, he took it across to Pavlenko.

"That should keep him busy for an hour or so," he whispered.

The barman retreated to his corner and soon went back to sleep.

Sokolov talked about the weather, his plans to return to Moscow, the prospects for peace. Dorothy played the game, engaging in lively conversation, while watching her adversary – or ally, she could still not decide – closely. After some fifteen minutes, Pavlenko had fallen asleep.

"Let's go somewhere more congenial," said Sokolov, leaning across the table and touching her hand, still in its leather glove.

"If you wish," she replied.

They went quietly upstairs and entered a bedroom – containing just a bed, bedside table, a lamp and a chair – at the end of a first-floor corridor.

"I assume it's bugged," said Dorothy, smiling.

"It's one of the few that is not. As I organise the eavesdropping around here, I get to choose."

"I'll take your words with a pinch of salt."

"I'll prove it," he replied, taking the bedside lamp apart, unscrewing the shaky ceiling light and emptying the drawer in the bedside table. "You see? There is nothing, not even under the bed."

She smiled.

"Dorothy, we have only a little time." He undid her coat and slipped it off her shoulders. He removed her jacket and unbuttoned her blouse. Barely able to control himself, he fondled her breasts and thighs.

"Shall we?" he whispered.

"Yes. I think we should," she replied.

He locked the door.

Quickly, they removed each other's remaining clothes, kissing hungrily as they did so. He almost threw her onto the bed and within seconds had penetrated her. They both came quickly. Afterwards, they lay side by side, each smoking a cigarette.

"What next, Colonel?"

"And that is also my question to you," he replied. "Do you wish to stay and serve our cause as I believe you do? Or are you going to persuade me to come to London?"

"What can you offer me if I stay, Colonel?"

"I could offer a good time in Moscow to a British traitor – one of their best officers, recruited by the Soviets right under their noses at Yalta."

Dorothy ran her manicured fingers across his lips.

"That's not enough for what I'm worth – not nearly enough. I play for high stakes. I want much more than that."

"I'm not sure what more I can offer." He paused. "Perhaps a Soviet medal if you tell me more of London's secrets, which I am certain you can."

"A medal is still not enough. We women are used to much more than trinkets like that."

"What more do you want?" he said in exasperation. "If it's more sex, I can give you plenty of that." He caressed her nipples.

"That's still not enough! Colonel, I am expensive – really expensive."

"Then what the hell do you want?"

"I want you to be my lover in London. I want you to spice up our sex with lots more of Uncle Joe's secrets. And I want you to bring the Eilers girl with you."

Sokolov was taken aback. "How can I do all that? You must be mad!"

"I'm not, Colonel. I'm deadly serious. Just think about it. Sex in London, a fine house in Mayfair, lots of other girls at your beck and call when I'm away – and of course long walks in the countryside so you can tell me your innermost secrets, including your connection with the *Abwehr*."

"I had none."

"Oh, I think you did. Perhaps long ago you had a German ancestor? But we can talk about it in London."

She whispered in his ear. His face went white.

"You wouldn't do that!"

"Try me, Colonel." She gently kissed his lips. "No more time for speaking. We have to go."

She felt him watching her as she sat on the side of the bed, slowly bending forward to put on her black stockings, the top of her breasts showing above her black camisole. After sliding into her skirt and slipping on her high heels, she equally slowly put on her blouse, her jacket and coat. She enjoyed the effect it was having on him. She could ask him to do anything.

"Hurry up, Colonel. If we don't get downstairs quickly, Pavlenko will wake up and your goose will be cooked. We have to do it – right now."

Before leaving the room Dorothy checked her appearance in the small wall mirror: clothing neat, her hair well groomed, she showed no sign of their recent sexual activity.

Downstairs, the Major resisted all of Sokolov's attempts to wake him. The barman stirred, his breath smelling of vodka. Sokolov removed the car keys from Pavlenko's tunic and gave the barman a couple of roubles for his trouble. They walked briskly to the car and, after Dorothy had given him a long lingering kiss, Sokolov held the door for her as she settled onto the back seat. He took the wheel and drove them to Soviet headquarters.

"Wait here," said Sokolov. "If I don't appear within fifteen minutes, you can assume it has all gone wrong."

After the Colonel got out, Dorothy opened her handbag and released the safety catch on the pistol.

Almost twenty minutes later, Sokolov reappeared – with a military guard almost dragging Karin Eilers behind him. She was handcuffed and blindfolded.

"Put her in the car, next to the woman," he shouted to the guard. "And then get in the car and drive."

"Where are you taking the prisoner, Colonel?"

"To her execution, you fool. Now get in. Hurry! Drive."

"But she wasn't sentenced to death. She was given hard labour."

"We've changed our minds. She's not worth the transport. Hurry man, hurry! Get into the damn driving seat."

The guard got in.

181

"Where's your authority, Colonel? I have to account for all those in my charge."

Sokolov tapped his epaulette. "Here, you idiot, here!" he shouted. "Now, drive. Follow my directions."

They sped away, the sentries saluting as they left the front gate heading for the centre of the city.

After a short distance, the road weaved between several large mounds of rubble. Dorothy ordered the driver to stop.

"Get out," she said in fluent Russian.

The guard looked at Sokolov.

"Yes," he confirmed. "Get out and start walking – in that direction. Do it now!"

The guard stumbled along the roadside for a few yards. Sokolov leapt from the car.

"No, idiot, go in that direction – towards that pile of rubble."

As Sokolov ran back to the car, Dorothy got out and, raising her pistol, took aim at the guard and fired.

"Put her in the boot. Quickly. I hear a vehicle coming."

Sokolov grabbed Karin from the rear seat and thrust her into the boot.

The car began to move. Dorothy was behind the steering wheel.

"Why the hell did you shoot him?"

"He had to go. He had heard and seen too much."

Neither spoke. Dorothy watched her rear-view mirror. No one seemed to be following. They approached the boundary between the Russian and US sectors. While there was no formal checkpoint, so permitting free and uncontrolled access in both directions, there were periodic checks by Russian and Allied military, mainly to suppress racketeering and other dubious activities. She looked ahead. There was a random check in place.

"Now, Colonel, this is the difficult part – a test of your skill. Your job is to talk us through the checkpoint. I'm your driver and we're on our way to an urgent meeting at the Kommandatura. Don't fail."

Sokolov looked nervous.

They took their place in the queue of vehicles. Sokolov, his face growing paler, had his pass ready and Dorothy hers – a fake Soviet military ID – to show through the window. They eased ahead towards the checkpoint. As the car was summoned forward, the guards – a mixture of Russian soldiers and police – seemed agitated, holding their guns in an aggressive posture. Dorothy edged the vehicle forward, still deciding whether to risk stopping or not. One of the policemen moved to the middle of the vehicle lane, motioning the car to stop in front of him. She decided what she had to do. She pressed her foot down on the brake, while pressing equally hard on the accelerator, to give the impression to the guard that she was having difficulty moving the car forward. A Russian soldier came towards her. As he did so, she took her foot off the brake and with her foot still hard down on the accelerator the car surged through the checkpoint and into the US sector. She stopped the vehicle, now surrounded by US soldiers.

Winding down the window she shouted, "I am a British officer and I have a Russian defector in the car. If you don't get out of the fucking way, one of those bastards over there will start firing and we'll all be dead. Just call British headquarters to say that Mrs Maddox is on her way with two important passengers."

She drove on past the astonished guards and onlookers. But instead of heading direct to Lancaster House, she went in another direction.

After a while she stopped the car. Sokolov sat beside her, his face drained.

"Valentin, your information was never good enough – until nearer the end when you fell for my bait and revealed much more than you intended about the extent of your penetration of our service. You did so because you thought I was in my heart a committed Communist, that I would finally join your side – that you would be able to bed me day after day. You thought of the pride you would feel, the kudos that would give you in Moscow – possessing a British agent as your whore. For a while, I was greatly tempted by your flattery, by the idea of being a double agent. And yes, the sex was good – its intensity, its roughness. I would have loved more. But in the end that would not have worked. We would have tired of one another, exhausted by the sexual demands placed on each other. Besides, you could never afford my price. As I said, I'm a highly expensive woman. Of course, the right thing to do now would be to interrogate you for more information about the identity of your agents in our service. But that's not going to be possible because you got to know too much about me and my beliefs – about how you almost tempted me to switch sides. You've said you are good at keeping secrets. But you're not. After two vodkas, you become loose-tongued. The more vodka I gave you the more I found out about you, the German ancestors and the intelligence you had about my country's secrets. I could never trust you to keep your mouth shut. So, we'll have to manage without you."

"I never asked for this outcome. I wanted you in Moscow. We would have made a powerful couple," said Sokolov.

"I'm afraid that's never going to happen, Valentin. You're finished and so am I. But I will go on to do something else. You won't. Goodbye, Colonel Sokolov."

She leaned across to kiss him and as she did so she pulled the trigger.

A little later she drove the car into British headquarters. She got out, pointed to the slumped body in the front passenger seat and urged the guards to release and take care of the terrified young woman in the boot. Ignoring requests for her to report immediately to Nolan and urgent calls from Blackstone, she went home and locked the door.

CHAPTER FOURTEEN

The Aftermath

The cover-up of the Sokolov affair began straightaway.

Within forty-eight hours Dorothy Maddox was back in London, suspended immediately from the service. No explanation was given in headquarters for her sudden return. The incident in Berlin went unreported in the British newspapers, largely on account of a D-notice requesting all editors not to publish any information about it since to do so would compromise highly sensitive operations at a time when the western sectors of the city were at peril from possible Soviet military action. The British mission in Berlin persuaded local news sources to do likewise, though what had happened near Friedrichstraße remained for some days a matter of gossip and innuendo until it was overshadowed by Russia's further tightening of its growing blockade of the road access to the three western sectors. Sokolov's body was discreetly restored to the Russians, who were equally keen to say nothing, to avoid embarrassment.

Dorothy never returned to 54 Broadway; all contact with her colleagues was severed. None called her at home. She knew that her incoming and outgoing telephone calls would be monitored. She had sealed her fate. She was consigned to an assumed name and a life of isolation – a woman living alone in a small detached house in rural Sussex with only a black cat for company. She earned a little income from occasional translation work and, under an additional pseudonym, writing articles for her local newspaper about gardening – the perfect cover for an agent who had sought to achieve single-handed the prize of turning an important Soviet agent and bringing him, or at least his information, back to London in order to reveal the identity of British traitors working for the Soviet Union. Her letter to her chief containing names of those sympathetic to Moscow was filed away, never acted upon.

Though lonely, she could not complain. In the still of the night, she often recalled that final encounter in Karlshorst, the breathless exhilaration of the danger to which she had exposed herself. Since Yalta, she had of her own volition crossed that final and extreme line, allowing her sexual allure and the excitement of physical intimacy with a handsome enemy, to whom she was fatally attracted, to be manipulated by her opponent, thus gravely compromising her loyalty to her service and country. She had all too often brushed that risk from her mind. Yet, as she dressed after Sokolov had made love to her at Karlshorst even more fiercely and forcefully than before, much to her intense pleasure, she finally realised that she could not bring herself to take that last irrevocable step into exile in Moscow and disgrace in London.

Confronted by this late realisation, the thrill of his penetration of her body had quickly drained away, exposing for the first time her self-deception, her hubris and the fatal, shameful flaw in her character. As they smoked and he fondled her sweet spot to rouse her again, she knew she had to turn back, not leap into the unknown. Whether on account of cowardice or shame or, she reflected, perhaps both, she had decided at the last minute to follow her conscience, at least by rescuing Karin Eilers from the misery her actions had inflicted upon her, and to kill her lover so that her dirty, traitorous secret would remain hidden. While her decision had meant Karin regained her freedom, she could not bring herself to seek the forgiveness of Richard Fortescue, whose confidence and friendship she had so grievously betrayed. She had often sat at her desk to write to him but the words to express what she wanted to say never came. It was too painful.

One night as she put the key in the front door of her empty, soulless house after an evening at the local theatre watching Shakespeare's *Julius Caesar*, she recalled the words of Brutus in Act 4:

> *There is a tide in the affairs of men*
> *Which taken at the flood leads on to fortune;*
> *Omitted, all the voyage of their life*
> *Is bound in shallows and in miseries.*
> *On such a full sea are we now afloat,*
> *And we must take the current when it serves,*
> *Or lose our ventures.*

Perhaps, she mused, as she bolted the door, if she had gone to Moscow, she might after all have possessed the power to change her life, to fulfil the philosophy with which, like so many others, she had flirted at university. By hesitating, by stepping back from the brink at the last moment, she had allowed the tide to ebb. Now, she was shipwrecked, stranded in shallow waters. Later, before turning out the bedside light, she looked at the small framed picture on her dressing table – not the one of her husband but that of Sokolov and her on the waterfront in Yalta, his arm around her waist. How different it might have been.

* * * * *

Helga Eilers survived the poison but its aftermath left her frail, a shadow of the woman who had once laughed with Eva Braun, who had adored Hitler. The German authorities, on strong British recommendation and with the concurrence of the US army war crimes unit, decided not to prosecute her. Any connection with the Sokolov business had to be buried. She was flown unobtrusively to West Germany to live in a one-room flat under a new name, an alleged war widow. She died three years later in obscurity, unreconciled with her daughter, with whom she had lost touch.

* * * * *

At her request, the British authorities in Berlin immediately flew Karin Eilers to Munich. Before her departure she was obliged to agree never to reveal the circumstances of her escape from Soviet captivity, in case – she was told – it might prejudice the fate of others in a similar predicament and, moreover, to avoid being pursued by Russian agents.

She found a job as a secretary in an import-export company and, after a while, did some occasional modelling of stockings for a women's clothing catalogue, her face never shown by her expressed wish. Gradually, the deep emotional scars of spending the closing months of the war as a prostitute in Munich and the ravages of her imprisonment in Karlshorst began to heal. Her regret at losing the much-read book that Fortescue had inscribed and given her, spitefully taken by one of the warders overseeing her solitary confinement, took longer to fade.

* * * * *

Major Richard Fortescue arrived at the War Office in Whitehall in June 1947. He had been asked to attend a private meeting with the Secretary of State for War, Frederick Bellenger, to receive an unconditional apology for the injustice done to him in Berlin. He was awarded an ex gratia payment and urged to consider remaining in the army, where he was likely to have a promising career. Fortescue declined, despite being pressed by Colonel Phillips to stay. Nor did he accept several offers to pursue a legal career outside of the army. Instead, he chose – at least temporarily – to return to his old school as a language teacher. But he found it hard to settle, his memories of Karin Eilers too potent. Susannah Thomas sought to renew their friendship following his exoneration but he said it would not be possible as he could never love her. A few months later she married someone else.

In the early spring of 1948, Fortescue, as restless as ever, accepted an invitation to teach English in Paris. He enjoyed his anonymity and being often alone, reflecting on the past and the future. Some evenings, after teaching, he liked to drift from bar to bar, watching the lives of others and politely turning away occasional advances from women who suggested he pay for their company. To them he would give a faint smile and gently wave away each approach in a discreet dismissive manner.

Two weeks after he arrived, a friend, Henri, took him to the Café de Flore on the corner of the boulevard Saint-Germain and the rue Saint-Benoît. On the left bank of the Seine, it was one of the city's oldest and most well-known cafés, taking its name from Flora, the goddess of flowers. After watching some late-afternoon fashion photography from their pavement table, they were joined by some of Henri's intellectual friends. The group of five included a striking young woman called Monique Pasquier. Tall and thin, her face with its large animated eyes and full lips framed by a shock of thick wavy shoulder-length hair, she constantly smoked and smiled. She asked why he was in Paris, about his past and what he sought from life. Exhausted – but pleasantly so – by his Bohemian inquisitor, he sought to uncover her past. She gave little ground, repeatedly turning the tables, much to his amusement. At the end of the evening, he and Monique shook hands. She hoped that the remainder of his stay in Paris would be enjoyable and rewarding.

A week later, with an hour or so to spare, he returned once more to the Café de Flore. Sitting at a table for one drinking coffee, as many often did, particularly women waiting to be noticed by a handsome young man, he flicked through a second-hand book he had just bought called *She Came to Stay*, written by the existentialist philosopher Simone de Beauvoir, an author Monique had previously described to him with evident knowledge. It was a thinly disguised fictional chronicle of a *ménage à trois* involving the author, her lover and fellow philosopher Jean-Paul Sartre, and a young woman. Absorbed by the book, Fortescue stayed at the café far longer than he had planned. He was about to leave when Monique suddenly appeared.

As she drew up a chair beside him, he noted how different she looked. Her hair was pinned up beneath a small hat and, unlike the loose-fitting trousers and top of a week ago, she wore a tight skirt and close-fitting jacket beneath a short, unbuttoned coat – the epitome of prevailing Paris chic. She confessed that she had often passed the café, in the hope he might be there so they could resume their earlier conversation. Impressed to see that he had bought de Beauvoir's book, Monique said she had met the author several times and had heard she intended to publish soon her new book, *The Second Sex*, in which she would reassert her opinion that women were as capable of choice as men and, that being the case, they could elevate themselves to a position in which they could choose their freedom.

Monique and Fortescue talked late into the evening. Now more intimate in disclosing her life, she said she was seventeen when the Germans invaded Paris. Throughout the occupation, and with her mother's encouragement, she had been one of the many young women, pretending still to be schoolgirls, running messages for the Resistance. She explained that this freedom to take risks had inspired her and others at the end of the war to do everything possible not to be pushed back into what de Beauvoir called "immanence" but instead to "transcend". Revealing that she worked as a secretary in a commercial office and confessing she was in a difficult relationship with a returned *maquisard*, whom she loved but who found it hard to accept that his lover was not always at home waiting for him, she said she was obliged to lead a double life, earning money on which to live but also, whenever possible, enjoying for a few hours the life of an independent Bohemian.

Fascinated by Monique, Fortescue invited her back to his room and she stayed the night. A week later she took him to an Édith Piaf concert where they sat arm in arm. Whenever they spent time together it was either at a café or in a museum, where they would steal a kiss when no one was looking, or in his bed.

Fortescue knew that his teaching job in Paris would have to end in June and with it would come the inevitable decision what to do next – to stay in Paris but do something different, to return to London, or to go somewhere else. He much enjoyed being with Monique, being her second lover, as she described him. It would be painful not to see her any more. Though she never admitted it, he began to suspect that she might even be falling in love with him. If that were so, and as long as he could not shake Karin from his mind, it would not be right to remain in Paris and mislead Monique as to his intentions. He still thought of Karin often and sometimes, when he was walking along a crowded street and glimpsed a tall, slim, dark-haired woman ahead of him, he would quicken his pace until he was alongside her, only to find it was not her after all.

At the beginning of May in that year, he met Max Steiner in Paris. They reminisced about old times in Nuremburg. Fortescue asked him about Karin. According to Steiner's information, she had returned to Munich. He had seen her once or twice in the street shortly afterwards but since then she had disappeared and not long after he was posted elsewhere.

"Why don't you go and find her, Rich?"

"I think I'm the last person she would want to see, if I were ever lucky enough to find her. I bought her a coffee and she ended up in a Soviet jail."

"My friend, either find her or forget her. Don't waste your life looking into the bottom of a whisky glass. You won't find her there. Besides, I think Monique has a big crush on you. You owe her an answer."

For a day or so, Fortescue thought about it. Searching for Karin would be like looking for the proverbial needle in a haystack. Then one morning he decided he would try. He broke the news of his departure to Monique. She replied that, though she was sad to see him leave after the happiness and respect he had brought to her life, it was his duty to go and find the woman he clearly still loved – to bring transcendence to her life. But if he did not find her she hoped he would return to hers.

Fortescue and Steiner flew together to Munich for old times' sake. Occasionally accompanied by Steiner, he spent over a week walking the streets, going to the opera, lingering in bars. With his money about to run out, he concluded that the woman he had loved was gone. He would never find her.

Ready to give up and to return to Paris and Monique, he sat alone in a bar near the cathedral, waiting for Steiner. It was late and one by one drinkers were drifting away into the night. He decided to have one last whisky as he listened to the pianist and violinist playing their remaining repertoire, a mix of jazz, ballads and traditional French tunes. They were joined on the platform by a middle-aged woman who sang a few songs cabaret style, her voice deep and mournful. She struck the mood of the vanishing evening.

"Now, gentlemen," she announced to an almost empty bar, "I will sing my last song. It's called *Marietta's Lied.*"

The tune and the opening poignant words made the memory of Karin even stronger.

> *Glück, das mir verblieb,*
> *Rück zu mir, mein treues Lieb.*
>
> *Joy, that near to me remains,*
> *Come to me, my true love.*

He asked the singer to sing it again.

As he listened, lost in the music, he felt a hand on his shoulder. He looked up. It was Steiner.

"I said I would come and find you here. There is someone to see you."

"Max, how many times have I told you – prostitutes are not my style. Send her away." He beckoned the singer to perform another encore.

"She's no prostitute," Steiner replied softly.

"I'll be the judge of that," replied Fortescue.

"Come on, Rich. Get a grip, man."

"In a minute, Max, I will in a minute. I must hear this song one more time."

He sipped his whisky, eyes closed, still mesmerised by the music.

"I gather you've been looking for me. Perhaps it's because you want your book back. It was taken from me in East Berlin, but I bought another copy, which you can have if you would like it."

He turned. It was her, just as he had first seen her in Munich all that time ago – dark shoulder-length hair, delicate lips and that faint smile. He couldn't find the words.

"Yes, it's me."

As they embraced, the singer, taking her cue, began to sing *Falling in Love Again* in the fashion of Marlene Dietrich.

* * * * *

As for the black notebook, it remains in Britain's secret archive, its contents still unrevealed.

AUTHOR'S NOTE

My diplomatic posting to Berlin from 1985–89 made an indelible impression on me.

Responsible for daily political liaison between the British Military Government (its formal title) and Berlin's civilian governing authority, I spent Monday to Friday each week in the Rathaus (town hall) Schöneberg, the seat of the city's administration in the western half of Berlin (the eastern half cut off by the Berlin Wall). Just a few steps away from my office was the balcony from which President John F. Kennedy delivered his famous *"Ich bin ein Berliner"* – "I am a Berliner" – speech on 26 June 1963, proclaiming America's unequivocal support for the city twenty-two months after the Russian-supported East Germany erected the infamous Wall to stop further mass immigration to the West. Another phrase in the President's speech was *"Lasst sie nach Berlin kommen"* – "Let them come to Berlin" – directed at those who claimed "We can work with the Communists."

In my office, used by previous British liaison officers from approximately 1948 onwards, were a few relics of earlier post-war years in Berlin, such as a radio, some old books and a few old files. But the ghosts of the past were ever-present after dark – the silent echoing corridors of the Rathaus, the cobbled dimly lit side streets close to the Reichsstraße (near where we lived) and the looming presence of the Olympic Stadium, scene of the 1936 Berlin Games. Periodically, my wife and I took it in turns to exercise Allied-right access to East Berlin. Crossing Checkpoint Charlie by car or on foot was relatively easy but arriving at Friedrichstraße in the East on the S-Bahn or U-Bahn was more challenging, particularly the latter, since the GDR *Grenzpolizei* did their best to get hold of our Allied identification cards – efforts we resolutely resisted. But this was small beer compared to some of the practical access difficulties the Western Allies faced in the period immediately following Germany's surrender and the division of Berlin into four military sectors: US, British, French and Russian. In that early period, the Allied liaison officers had to cross daily into the Russian sector to reach their respective offices in the

Neues Stadthaus in Parochialstraße because the Rotes Rathaus –
the red town hall, named after its red brick and the city's original
pre-war seat of local government – had been too severely
damaged to be used. In due course, the daily crossing became so
problematic that it was decided in the late 1940s to establish more
secure offices in Rathaus Schöneberg.

In my years as the British liaison officer I was responsible on
behalf of the British Military Government for monitoring
contacts between the Berlin government and the East Berlin
authorities, often in connection with the Berlin Wall, just as my
US and French colleagues were. We barely encountered the
Russians on account of their insistence that the GDR was
sovereign in East Berlin; if we had a problem, we should
approach the East German government. The Allies did not
agree, arguing that Berlin was legally still under post-war four-
power control and that therefore the proper channel for such
contacts was through the Russians. Despite their insistence that
the four-power control of Berlin was a thing of the past, the
Russians undermined their own case. They deployed a daily
military guard on the Soviet War Memorial in West Berlin;
were present daily in the Berlin Air Safety Centre, guaranteeing
or not – depending on their political mood – the safety of
British, US and French civilian flights between West Berlin and
West Germany; and in every fourth month of the year mounted
guard at Spandau Prison where Rudolf Hess, sentenced at the
Nuremburg war crimes tribunal to life imprisonment, remained
the sole prisoner. While my wife and I were in Berlin, she was
the deputy governor of Spandau Prison, as well as being the
legal adviser to the British Military Government.

There was another aspect of Russian activity designed to
demonstrate their ultimate political and military control in the
eastern part of Berlin. All Allied personnel, whether military or
diplomatic, were required to pass through Soviet checkpoints at
Dreilinden (on arriving in or leaving West Berlin) and likewise
at Helmstedt on the West German border, a procedure
completed in a most precise way. On each occasion, a Royal
Military Police sergeant would laboriously complete and issue a
formal laissez-passer. Proceeding to a wooden shed immediately

beyond the West Berlin boundary, we submitted the laissez-passer for scrutiny by a faceless official behind a screen, pushing it through a letter box for his examination. Once it had been stamped and returned through the same letter box, we drove on to a sentry hut and, with a military salute, presented the document to the Russian soldier for further inspection. Only then were we able to begin our journey.

One other feature that left a deep impression on me was the weekly Saturday market on the Straße des 17. Juni (named in commemoration of the 1953 East German uprising and known before 1953 as Charlottenburger Chaussee), a mile or so from the Brandenburg Gate. Going early most weeks to browse, it was there that I found a British passport issued on 3 October 1853 by the then British Foreign Secretary, Lord Clarendon, to Mr Robert Whitfield, to enable him and his wife and son to travel from Britain through the German states. That passport helped to inspire my trilogy of Herzberg novels. From time to time I also found German newspapers from the 1930s, such as the issue reporting in large front-page headlines Hitler's triumphant return to Berlin following the Munich Agreement with Neville Chamberlain in 1938; and later issues reporting on German setbacks in the war; and a copy of *Der Tagesspiegel* for 6 October 1946. But most thought-provoking was a print of post-war Berlin, in the vicinity of the famous Kaiser Wilhelm Memorial Church – the original church, built on the site in the 1890s, was badly damaged in an Allied bombing raid in 1943. The image is of hunched figures set in a dark, dismal, devastated city; hunger, weariness, mistrust and betrayal are palpable, a city still haunted by the shadows and echoes of the previous regime.

I have been back to Berlin innumerable times since 1989 – my wife and I still have many friends there – but it is against the backdrop of this particular picture and my vivid, lasting memories of Berlin before the fall of the Wall in November 1989 that I decided to write *The Executioner's House*.

Edward Glover
North Norfolk
Tuesday, 27 June 2017

ACKNOWLEDGEMENTS

I wish to thank several people who helped with this story.

My first and special thanks go to my loyal researcher, Jenny Langford, who kindly checked facts, uncovered ones I did not know and who patiently read my first draft. My warm thanks also go to my copy-editor, Sue Tyley, who, as with my previous books, reviewed the final manuscript for grammar and punctuation, inconsistencies and anomalies. I also wish to thank my long-standing friends in Berlin, Bianca and Jürgen Freymuth-Brumby, for kindly filling the gaps in my knowledge of the city in the early years after Germany's defeat. My gratitude also goes to my friends Cynthia Butterworth and Duncan Stuart, both formerly of the Foreign Office, and Lieutenant Colonel Anthony Le Tissier, a close and much-respected former Berlin colleague and British governor of Spandau Prison, for their essential advice on some aspects of the story; and to Professor Patrick Salmon, Chief Historian at the Foreign and Commonwealth Office, for providing additional advice on the British administrative structure in post-war Berlin.

I also wish to thank my graphic designer, Niall Cook, for his important and much-appreciated contribution to the book's presentation and production, and Julia Rafferty, an accomplished photographer, for her contribution to the cover image.

Last but not least, I wish to thank my wife, Audrey, for her support and encouragement, spurring me to stick to my crazy self-imposed target of writing this book in four months in the midst of many other pressing tasks. While it is not an experience I wish to repeat, I am nonetheless relieved that I adhered to my timetable, in keeping with my long-ingrained Foreign Office experience of meeting immutable ministerial deadlines.

ABOUT THE AUTHOR

Edward Glover was born in London in 1943. After gaining a history degree followed by an MPhil at Birkbeck College, London University, he embarked on a career in the British diplomatic service, during which his overseas postings included Washington DC, Berlin, Brussels and the Caribbean. He subsequently advised on foreign ministry reform in post-invasion Iraq, Kosovo and Sierra Leone. For seven years he headed a one-million-acre rainforest-conservation project in South America, on behalf of the Commonwealth Secretariat and the Guyana Government.

With an interest in 16th- and 18th-century history, baroque music and 18th-century art, Edward was encouraged by the purchase of two paintings and a passport to try his hand at writing historical fiction.

Edward and his wife, former Foreign & Commonwealth Office lawyer and leading international human rights adviser Dame Audrey Glover, now live in Norfolk, a place that gives him further inspiration for his writing. Edward sits on the board of trustees of the Welsh environmental charity Size of Wales and is vice-chairman of the Foreign & Commonwealth Office Association, an associate fellow of the University of Warwick's Yesu Persaud Centre for Caribbean Studies and a board member of The King's Lynn Preservation Trust.

When he isn't writing, Edward is an avid tennis player and – at the age of 71 – completed the 2014 London Marathon, raising £7,000 for Ambitious about Autism.

Printed in Great Britain
by Amazon